Rembrandt Redux

Rembrandt Redux

HUGO UYTTENHOVE

authorHOUSE®

AuthorHouse™
1663 Liberty Drive
Bloomington, IN 47403
www.authorhouse.com
Phone: 1-800-839-8640

First published by AuthorHouse   01/10/2011

ISBN: 978-1-4685-3885-4 (sc)
ISBN: 978-1-4685-3884-7 (hc)
ISBN: 978-1-4685-3883-0 (ebk)

Library of Congress Control Number: 2011963734

Printed in the United States of America

ALSO BY HUGO UYTTENHOVE:

Grand Scale Larceny:
They Heist of the Flemish Primitives (2010)

ACKNOWLEDGEMENT

This book is based on a screenplay written as a member of Writers Boot Camp. I would like to thank Mark Sable for his guidance in working out the kinks of the screenplay which smoothed the way to converting it to book form. I am thankful for the editing done by Robert Slentz-Kesler and especially by Kristin Conrad.

Raleigh, December 2011

AUTHOR'S NOTES

Dutch and German words are italicized. In those cases where the text doesn't offer immediate clarification, these words as well as historically relevant facts are explained below.

Brit milah: The Jewish ceremony of male circumcision

Damrak: A famous street in Amsterdam where ships moored on the canal at the dam

Florin: Once the monetary unit of The Netherlands and equivalent to 'Guilder'

Gracht: A canal in Dutch cities. The use of the word is replaced by 'canal' in the rest of the book.

Jenever: A typical Dutch alcoholic spirit akin to gin

Mach' schnell: Do it quickly

Oude Kerk: The *Oude Kerk* or Old Church was built in the heart of Amsterdam in 1250 and was originally called the Church of St. Nicolas. A new church was built around 1400 near the Dam.

Raus: Get out

Strafprozeßordnung: German code of criminal procedure

The Sortie: Rembrandt named this painting *The Sortie* representing a captain and his guardsmen ready to leave. Later it became known as the Night Watch, a misnomer since the light in the painting belies daylight from above.

Part I

REMBRANDT

[Rembrandt Harmenszoon van Rijn, painter, 1606-1669]

CHAPTER 1

Amsterdam

A morning in February 1647

THE NURSEMAID HAD given up trying to keep the children quiet as she feared the displeasure of her master who was still in bed and did not want to get up any time soon. In the middle of the winter the sun didn't come up until half past eight. It was rare for children to be outside at this time as they would normally be sitting around a small stove with its red potbelly warming up the single schoolroom. On this Sunday morning, before church services in the Reformed Church, Titus, the master's spoiled child had been begging to go outside. From his bedroom window on the second floor, overlooking the Breestraat near the Jewish Quarter, Titus had noticed the guard with a small lantern walking far away to the left of their mansion, not on the street, but on the *gracht* in front of the St. Antoniusstraat. Titus had heard his father mention a few weeks before that when a guard walks the canals, it meant only one thing: it was so cold that the water was frozen and people would be walking on the canal. It didn't happen every winter, but this year, there was a good chance because the wind kept coming from the north. Seeing the guard on the canal, Titus had gotten so excited that by eight o'clock he was already putting skates on his little boots, tightening them with leather straps. Geertje let him out to join the other children, and soon they were all skating, bumping into each other and falling, causing them to shriek and laugh loudly with their sounds traveling easily to van Rijn's bedroom.

Geertje Dircx did not have much patience this morning, not with the child and not with her master. She told the children repeatedly to keep it down, but having no command over them but one, the other children from the neighborhood felt free to skate up and down the canal, going under the bridges they usually crossed on their way to school. The cries of joy were unstoppable. It was a pure children's paradise without adult supervision and with the freedom to skate away from their neighborhoods since the canals connected vast areas of the city. Geertje had told one of the older girls to tell Titus to come back in the house when the church bells announced half past nine. She would have to get him ready for the ten o'clock service, providing his father would also be ready. Back inside the house, Geertje was going through a chest of jackets and picked the one Titus would wear for the services. She didn't particularly mind making noise because she wanted the master to get up. She called his name a few times, but he had the pillow wrapped around his head to drown out the noise from the canal.

She collected the other Sunday clothes for the boy and went into the master's bedroom. Even though the room was cold, she knew that the master was warm in the small bed, lying on the soft cotton mattress and covered with several layers of wool blankets. Although he had a large fireplace installed, he never used it because he didn't want to do the upkeep. Since Geertje was only there to take care of Titus, and the master could not afford another maid, the two oak logs in the basket had been there for over three years. She approached the side of the bed and smelled the warm air coming from his uncovered shoulder. Almost immediately, her memory of one night, now about a year ago, was triggered. Her master had just received a payment for one of his *Passion* paintings, and he had been celebrating by spending money all day. He had bought a new bed for Titus, a set of larger pots for the kitchen, and a lot of paint and materials for his atelier, located next door. He wasn't usually a big drinker, but along with a good beer, he had quite a few *jenevers* that night with his friends on the *Damrak*. He returned to the house around ten at night and he called her into his bedroom. She remembered the coziness and the comfort of the bed, his strong arms, but also his gentle strokes and firm command during their love making. She had pitied him. She was much older than him, and perhaps she was just as eager as he was, but the thought that this man had lost not only three of his four children shortly after birth, but also his wife at age thirty, was enough for her to submit to his need. Much to her chagrin, not since that one memorable night had he asked her again to share in what he called the pleasures of the flesh. Later, she had modeled for semi-nude paintings several times, but he had never regarded that as an invitation for her to join him in this cozy nest again.

Standing near his bed, she let him know that he had fifteen minutes more, and then he had to get up. God knows how late he had been working in his atelier again last night she wondered. If only his time spent there would give him an equal proportion of income so he could live more like the neighbors, with new clothes for Titus once in a while. She had overheard him many times complaining about not having money for the upkeep of the mansion. She wasn't even sure he could afford the mansion at all, and she had heard rumors that he owned money to the lenders. Her own mother had warned her about working for artists who had so many ups and downs that she would share both the lives of the haves and the have-nots without much pity or sympathy from others. If only he married her, she thought again, he'd be at peace and paint more, rather than letting his students put the paint on the canvas.

The smell of heated milk was wafting through the alcove when Rembrandt walked into the kitchen. He checked the pan, and with a wooden spoon fished out the thin layer of milky skin which he put the skin on a piece of bread already lightly smeared with salted lard. He took a bite and looked for something to drink. The milk was for Titus, his only son, so he poured himself a glass of water from the tin can sitting on a small table. He was still wearing a night shirt that was partially propped into his pants and partially hanging out in the back. He had pulled woolen socks over the bottom of his pants and shuffled over to the table. He called out for Geertje. She was in the bedroom checking on Titus from the opened window. She pondered whether or not to start the conversation about money before services. Her master was not particularly short-tempered when confronted by criticism. He was, however, as frustrated as she was when clients did not pay him enough for his work, or worse, did not pay at all because there was a dispute. She decided to wait until after services when Titus would be back on the canal.

She entered the kitchen area and Rembrandt turned to her.

"Ah, there you are. The milk's getting cold. Is Titus out there with those rotten kids?"

"He'll be in soon, don't worry."

"Couldn't they have waited to go out until after services?"

"You know how it is. This is the first day and they have been waiting since New Year's Day."

"I need my sleep if I'm to do my work," he said, rubbing his eyes. "By the way, after services I am visiting with Mr. Huygens."

"Does he have a new order from the Stadhouder, our Prince?"

Rembrandt gulped the water from his cup, washing down the last of the bread and wiped his mouth with his sleeve.

"Maybe. I'll see."

The *Oude Kerk* was about ten minutes from van Rijn's house. Titus couldn't wait to leave after the long and boring service. It was almost noon but it wasn't hunger that drove him outside. It was the thought of binding those skates on again and getting the ice chair out for more fun on the canals. Rembrandt himself wanted to wait a while until the nobles seated in the front of the center nave had left. Many of them provided work for him and his atelier. He was sure that Huygens had already gone, but he hadn't spotted him. Better to let him get home before I get to his house on the *Herengracht*, he thought. Rembrandt finally nodded to Geertje that it was all right for her and Titus to leave. His eyes followed them to the back of the church until they were out of sight. When he was sure that everyone had left the church, he wandered to the back where his beloved Saskia was buried. He liked being alone standing at the foot of the white, marble slab worked almost seamlessly into the church's black, tiled floor. Like most churchgoers, Calvinists and Reformed Protestants, Rembrandt was dressed in black. His coat was accented with dark gray velour and his wide pants were tucked into black leather boots. A simple white collar contrasted with his clothes.

He wore a dark blue hat with a small feather of a blue jay in it. His feet were cold but he didn't complain because style trumped discomfort. He wore black woolen gloves and held his prayer book close to his chest.

At the back of the church he leaned against a huge pillar that was part of the central nave structure. The weak winter sun splashed its light from the left side over several flat gravestones. There was no inscription on the marble slab in front of him, because he had requested the undertaker not to carve the name of the love of his life into the marble. After several years, it still pained him to see her name, and it was sufficient for him to know that she rested here. Many years from now, he thought, nobody would remember who was buried here, and that was fine. This way, Saskia would remain his and only his. He was thankful she had left him Titus as a part of her. Fighting tears welling up, he slowly gazed up at the wooden ceiling and the bright paintings that survived the iconoclast events when the reformists rose up against the pope and destroyed statues and religious icons eighty years ago. He shook his head thinking that this was once a proud Catholic church. He cast his gaze back on the marker, slowly sank to his knees, rested his hands on the cold marble, and kissed the stone.

Rembrandt walked briskly along the *Warmoesstraat* to the *Damrak*. In his mind he was rehearsing the things he would say to Huygens, depending on what transpired at the luncheon. Could he be so bold as to hope that the Stadhouder was finally paying up for the last paintings? If he did, that would make it easier to accept the next assignment. If he didn't, and the request would be another painting, he would have to be tactful in his refusal, because undoubtedly there would be other people at the lunch table and he did not want to scare off any present and future customers.

When he crossed the *Singel* toward the *Herengracht*, the crowd on the canal was larger than the one in the street. He paused for a moment on the bridge watching skaters, parents and children alike. Several were standing near a small table where a woman was selling buckwheat waffles. The smell carried by the smoke from a small fire near the table stirred his stomach. He hurried on to Huygens's house. He was hoping for a great lamb stew and the new coffee from the islands.

CHAPTER 2

Amsterdam
An afternoon in February 1646

C ONSTANT HUYGENS WAS the personal secretary of the Stadhouder Prince Frederik Hendrik of Orange, and was himself a powerful man in Amsterdam. He knew most wheelers and dealers in the trade business, and Holland as a nation was doing very well. Most of the traders worked with the Dutch East Indies Company which had a monopoly on business with Asian countries, but some offered their services in other countries. He, like most of the hard working people in the city, was well aware of their trading bases in Japan at Dejima, and on the African Gold coast in Elmina. Ships brought spices and especially salt gathered from the large salt ponds from the Caribbean Island of St. Maarten. Many of the conversations at the luncheons were centered on the good fortunes of their shipping empire. Being good Calvinists, they often included in their discussions the benefits they bestowed upon the lower classes. Behind the scenes however, the feel-good attitude was tainted with a dark secret. The common man did not know that once those salt ships unloaded in the port of Amsterdam, they went to Elmina where they picked up slaves destined for the Caribbean and the Americas. The traders who were in the know didn't talk about it and were careful to limit their comments on their business to basics. If asked about the half-empty ships that left the port of Amsterdam, their standard response was that they picked up African hardwoods to top off the cargo holds. Huygens controlled the conversation today, so it would not be about the spice trade, but rather on the current events in the Low Countries.

Rembrandt handed his coat and gloves to the housemaid. As was customary, he kept his hat on. When he entered the dining room of the double-wide house in the trading district, he recognized everyone. Four well dressed men with lace collars were benefactors of his. Two of them had posed and paid him very well upon the completion of *The Sortie*, his largest painting to date. He had painted Frans Cocq as the central figure, and Willem van Ruytenberg, off the Cocq's left in the forefront of the painting. They had recently confided in him that they didn't particularly like the painting. Rembrandt had questioned them as to how they came to that conclusion, and discovered that they based it on negative comments they heard from others. Rembrandt knew about the rumors spread by a few dissatisfied customers. They were the tough ones to get money from because they claimed he hadn't portrayed them clearly enough. He had no choice but to sue those customers in court. He had two cases pending against Rombout Kemp and Jacob Dircksen. Luckily they were not at Huygens's house. As usual, a savvy Huygens was well aware of the situation and had handpicked his guests. He greeted Rembrandt.

"Welcome. We're just about to sit down."

"Glad my timing is right," Rembrandt said, slightly nodding to the other guests.

"How's Titus? Is he making progress in his drawings?"

"No. I don't think he'll be a painter."

Huygens pulled out a chair next to his. "Well, I'm sure he'll grow up to be a fine, young man. Please be seated."

By the time the maids brought in the first course, everyone had taken their place at the table. Rembrandt knew that Huygens wanted to talk to him in private. Why else would he have been seated next to him at the head of the long table?

When the conversation drifted to the other side of the table, Huygens turned to Rembrandt.

"I have good news for you."

"From the Stadhouder?"

"Yes."

"Another painting?"

"No, not this time. Although he's very pleased with the six *Passion* paintings and the last one entitled *The Circumcision of Christ*. He has completed the decoration of the *Noordeinde Palace* in The Hague."

"So, what's the good news?"

"He's sending his treasurer tomorrow at noon to your house with the payment for the last two paintings."

"The Lord be praised! Is he paying the full amount?"

"Yes, I was told it would be 2,400 florins."

"Then that settles the dispute. I am pleased."

"I thought you would be."

"But why now? I've been waiting a year for this."

"Apparently last week he had an important visitor from Portugal."

"A Jew I presume? We seem to be getting many Jewish refugees. I heard about the relentless persecution by the pope's men over there."

"Yes, you're right on all counts."

"So who was the visitor?"

"A rabbi, Menassah Ben Israel. The Stadhouder showed him your last painting and the rabbi praised it during his entire visit. At one point, the Stadhouder jokingly said that the man in the painting looked a little like the rabbi. From then on, the Stadhouder seemed to value your painting more."

"And so he figured he'd finally pay up?"

"I don't question him. That painting is now his favorite."

"Well, that leaves me with just a few dispute cases."

"You'll be doing all right. Your work is well liked."

"I hear that Amalia, his wife is the real collector in the family."

"She likes Rubens too, and if Frederik Hendrik doesn't stop her soon, he won't be able to pay any more bills."

CHAPTER 3

Bensberg
An evening in March 1754

THE COLD WIND raced around the sturdy walls of the castle, whistling sharply in short tones around the square corners, and then it jumped into the valley below taking the sound with it. Years ago, in the town of Bensberg, about fifteen kilometers from Köln, one of the first Dukes of Palatine had his primary residence built as a castle. The current Duke had its robust structure modernized into a more Renaissance style fortress, popular at that time in France. When criticized by the Duchess, he would usually respond with the observation that he, or rather they, without a doubt, deserved this opulent dwelling since he had increased the family fortune twenty-fold in less than ten years. Trading with large Dutch companies had given him indeed unique and much needed supplies his associates sold all over Germany, even as far as Hungary. He was able to amply supplement his main business of running part of the Habsburger Empire. That by itself earned him a sizable income. Of course, he had a great start. He had inherited a fair amount of money from the Dukes of Bavaria, and in his latest function as Elector Palatine, his fortune had been a guarantee to power and wealth. Since the country was not at war, and there were no enemies to worry about, he had done away with the defense towers, covered part of the moat, and spent huge sums of money on the extravagant interior and made special places for all his collections.

The Duke slowly made his way upstairs. Paintings of his ancestors lined the grand staircase. Five generations had left their mark. There wasn't a day he didn't look at the paintings. At the bottom of the steps was a large painting of Amalia von Solms-Braunsfeld who was married to Prince Frederik Hendrik of Orange. Often, the Duke had wondered why the prince hadn't become king of The Netherlands. Amalia herself had a lot of power after her husband died. Politically savvy, she knew that she had to marry off her children to rising royalty. Her son married the daughter of King Charles I of England, and her daughters married German princes. She passed on the titles, privileges and honors that came with being a Stadhouder to her son Willem II and, when he died, to her grandson Willem III. One thing she did not pass on however, was the wealth in the form of art. When she moved back to her home country, she had the entire collection moved to Germany. Apparently, his assumed great grandfather Philip Willem of Palatine-Neuberg, whose painting hung next to Amalia's, had inherited over three hundred paintings. Over time, Philip Willem had to sell some to keep his lifestyle intact, but he certainly had kept the best.

The painting of his assumed grandfather Johan Willem II was stunning. He looked like a French King, a red cape draped from his shoulders to the floor, and trimmed with fine white ermine fur. The copper plate on the edge of the gilded frame read Elector Palatine, 1558-1716. He had not known him of course, but heard much about him. He was the one who added the chapel to the castle off the east wing, next to the kitchens. The chapel was similar to many chapels of those days with the then popular yellow pastel color on the walls. Being protestant, he went with the times, so there were no niches or supports for statues of saints. Upon moving into the castle the Duke had hung seven Rembrandts in the Chapel with the *Raising of the Cross* above the simple altar.

At the first landing he stood in front of the painting of his assumed father Charles Philip III. The Duke smiled. He had never known him, and when Charles Philip III died in 1742, having no heirs and being the last in his family line of the Palatines, his will revealed that he, Duke Charles Theodore was somehow his illegitimate son. His mother had claimed having no knowledge of the Elector Palatine and denied ever having met him. Nevertheless, she did not object to her son becoming the successor of the Dukes of Palatine. After taking a few deep breaths, Charles walked the last set of steps toward his bedroom. Before becoming the new Elector Palatine he already had the title of Duke of Bavaria. Since this castle was his inheritance he had used it as his playground, away from the Bavarian courts. It would be in his family for a long time. He closed the door to his bedroom and pulled the curtains at the windows overlooking the courtyard.

At first the dark sky swallowed small puffs of the orange glow, letting the wind take any fleeting remnants away, but after a short while the glow turned into streaks of yellow and red, and the night could no longer hide the stirring cauldron below. Soon, a solid curtain of fiery colors rose up faster and higher and if viewed from the nearby hilltop, the chapel at the northeast corner of the castle was capped by a most eerie canopy of fire.

The night watchman crossing the dark courtyard saw the first flames coming through a window, his attention drawn by breaking glass behind him. After a moment of stunned silence, he sounded the alarm. His loud yells of "*Feuer! Wasser und schnell!*" were soon answered by servants who were carrying buckets of water. Within a minute, the Duke himself appeared. He ran for the chapel with the key in his hand. When he opened the double solid wood doors, each decorated with a large carved version of the Bavarian and Palatine family shields, he immediately jumped back when the flames, fanned by the cold air rushing in, lashed out at him. Once the fire seemed to settle back inside, he took a filled bucket, walked back into the door opening and threw the water on the pews. He had to step back as the wind sucked the smoke into the courtyard. After two more buckets the Duke saw that most of the altar and the roof were burning, as well as the pews to one side. Damn the candles, he thought, and kept calling for water as the drapery behind the altar was burning, setting the frame of the large painting on fire. There were plenty of servants bringing the water, but no one else was helping to put out the fire. He yelled for others to go inside and get the paintings off the walls. Two men jumped in after they were doused by water, and in the thick smoke they each yanked a painting off a wall. The Duke took the altar piece himself and carried it into the courtyard with the others. All three went in for another painting. As they returned a third time, they saw that the roof had collapsed near the door and that most pews had caught fire. The smoke was so thick, they couldn't breathe. The Duke ran back outside and swore, having lost the last painting.

Inside the chapel, one of the housemaids entered from the hallway connected to the kitchen. She held a wet burlap bag over her head and in front of her nose and mouth. She quickly moved to the painting hanging near the door. The top of the frame was already burning. She did not hesitate. She took the piece of art off the wall, and ran with it into the kitchen. Using the bag, she put out the flames burning the bottom of the frame and the left side of the canvas. She heard the Duke yell like a madman. Without further hesitation, she put the painting in the bag. She carefully stretched and smoothed the bag so the entire frame was covered. She then quickly ran to a small reception room which had access to a terrace. She opened the door, stepped outside and walked from the terrace across the gardens to the open fields in the valley, where she vanished with the wind.

CHAPTER 4

Moitzfeld
Later that evening in March 1754

IT WAS ONLY a half hour walk from the castle at Bensberg to the small village Rachel was born in. She did not meet anyone on the road which was good because they may have stopped her, asking what that smell was, coming from the burlap bag. She had noticed it herself as soon as she left the terrace; burnt wood and another strong odor. She had finally figured it out. It must have been the paint. She panicked because in the hurry she had not looked carefully at the painting. If it was burned, the congregation would not be happy. She stopped after she had made sure that there was nobody following her. When she took it out of the bag, in the faint light of the moon she saw the entire face of the man and his upper body and the baby on his lap. She must have taken it just in time because everything appeared black just above the head and all along the left side and bottom left corner. She put the damaged painting back in the bag and walked on.

She had been a kitchen maid for about three years at the castle. It was hard work, day in and day out. Even when the Duke was away in Bavaria, guests came to stay at the castle and she worked long days. Unless there was something urgent with her family in town, she was allowed only one Sunday afternoon each month off. Those Sunday afternoons she visited her parents. They were always pleased when she brought something from the castle. Often Rabbi Ariel Israel was at the house talking about life in the old days when his parents moved from Holland to Germany. He had told them stories about how generations ago his family came from Portugal to find refuge in Holland together with many Jewish countrymen. The Dutch had been very kind to them and they settled in Amsterdam, where the patriarch of the family became the rabbi at the synagogue in the city. That rabbi's son told his own son about his father's fascination with a single painting that he had seen at a palace. He had offered to buy it, but the owner did not want to part with it. Apparently this was a very powerful man and he liked his paintings so much that he built special rooms for them. A few years after that man died, the rabbi met the man's secretary who told him that the man had decided that upon his death, the painting should be given to the synagogue. Unfortunately, the man's wife had it moved to her family estate in Germany, and taken the painting with her. So the story went, as it was passed from father to son over the years.

Rabbi Ariel Israel had been told the story about a painting named *The Circumcision* many times. Imagine his surprise when he went to the castle one day and the Duke showed off his paintings. The moment he had entered the chapel he knew that this was the painting in the story. It had to be. So he had asked the Duke how he got the painting and the Duke had answered that he inherited it with the castle. Most of the castle's art had come from Holland, the Duke had explained, and pointed out that those in the chapel were all Rembrandts. The rabbi had realized that the painting's provenance was confirmed. An amazing coincidence one might have thought, but the rabbi thought it was Divine Providence. Afterwards he had lamented to Rachel and her parents that the painting was not in the rightful hands. It belonged in his own family, to his own congregation.

Rachel had remembered the rabbi's kvetch well. To be sure, the rabbi had never suggested that she ask the Duke for it, let alone steal it. Tonight, however, she saw an opportunity that demanded quick and decisive action. She did the right thing and surely, the rabbi would be very pleased indeed to have this painting. She couldn't wait to give it to him as she approached the first houses of the town of Moitzfeld, and held the bag close to her body. It was dark and the single street lantern was unlit, but she knew her way very well. She counted the houses and knew that she would be at the rabbi's house on Hofstrasse at any moment. At the corner she looked one more time behind her but only the wind stroked her face. She was relieved that nobody had followed her, and she knocked on the door.

Rabbi Ariel Israel was a middle-aged, gentle giant of a man. When his wife brought Rachel to him in his small study, he got up and towered over the two women. He took her hand and gently rested his left hand on her shoulder.

"Shalom, Rachel," he smiled. "What a surprise to see you here. Is all well with your parents?"

"Yes, they're fine. At least I think they are," she answered.

He pointed to a chair. "Well, sit down *Fraulein*, and tell me what I can do for you," he said and turned to his wife. "Get us some sweet beer, will you dear?"

He sat down across from Rachel. She moved the burlap bag from the side of the chair in front of her so that it rested in between them.

"I came from the castle, rabbi."

"So late at night? I hope nothing serious happened."

"There was a fire. The chapel burned down."

"Oh no, that's terrible." He stood up and walked toward a small window. He turned around and sighed. "Did those beautiful paintings burn? Tell me it isn't so."

Rachel trembled a bit. She realized that she hadn't rehearsed her story very well, so she decided to tell him what she knew and why she had done what she did.

"I heard the yelling and screaming in the courtyard as I was finishing up in the kitchen. I looked outside but saw nothing. Then suddenly someone was getting water from the well and there were several men running to the chapel. Then I saw it. The flames were shooting through the roof and I heard the slate cracking and falling in the courtyard."

The rabbi's wife came in and the rabbi took a glass and gave it to Rachel. "Here drink something. Go on, what happened then?"

"I heard the Duke yelling about the paintings and saw people run inside the chapel. I went into the hall off the kitchen and wanted to help. I took a wet burlap bag, put it over my head and ran into the chapel through the side door. I vaguely saw the Duke and two other men run outside, each with a painting. There was one painting left and I wanted to help. I took it from the wall and ran with it to the kitchen.

I was going to give it to the Duke, but then I heard him yell and swear that it was too late for the last painting and that they couldn't get in and that it was surely burned. When I saw the painting I had taken, I knew I had to bring it here."

Rachel held up the bag and handed it to the rabbi.

"My child, what an ordeal, but why bring it here? It belongs to the Duke and he may reward you for saving it."

"But you told us it belongs to your family, our congregation."

"Rachel, listen, the story about the painting has been passed down through the years. Yes, maybe it is ours, and God knows how I was overjoyed to see it at the castle. It was good enough to know where it was and that I could see it almost any time I wanted to. You must know that this is not yours to take. You should take it back first thing in the morning."

Rachel raised the painting from the bag. The left side and bottom were severely damaged and the frame was ruined. She turned the front of the painting to the rabbi.

"Look, rabbi. I understand what you're saying, but look at this man in the painting. He's family. He's one of us. We were promised that painting, just like God promised us the land of Israel. God in all his wisdom has surely guided me tonight and returned this painting to its rightful owner. You told my parents several times that it should have been given to your family. Well, here it is. God's justice."

The rabbi shook his head and looked at his wife. He sat down again and stared at the old bearded man in the picture: a gentle giant like himself, with a little baby on his lap. Tears welled up in his eyes.

"The man who painted this understood *Brit milah*."

Rachel and the rabbi's wife had cast their eyes down and knew not to speak.

The rabbi stood up again.

"I will go to visit the Duke tomorrow. He must know about this."

He took a prayer shawl and hung it over his shoulder, letting the long ends hang down in front of him.

"For now, let's pray."

The women stood up and they bowed their heads.

"Praised are you, Adonai our God, King of the Universe, who commanded us in the ritual of circumcision through the covenant with Abraham, our father."

The rabbi put his hand on Rachel's shoulder and continued.

"Adonai, we thank you for protecting your daughter Rachel for saving this living symbol from destruction. May she forever be in your favor."

CHAPTER 5

Düsseldorf
A morning in April 1919

F IVE MONTHS HAD passed since the Great War. The Treaty of Versailles had been signed between the allied forces and members of the new German government. Peace had returned to Europe. It was a forced peace however, and the German generals had never officially surrendered, at least not in person. Sending civilians to the peace conference had been a perfect way to avoid blame for losing the war or be tried in various European courts for the use of chlorine gas. The civilian government had inherited a disaster of a previously unknown scale. Any semblance of both economic and military power was gone by virtue of the loss of the coal region of Alsace-Lorraine and the restrictions on military forces in the New Republic. Not that it would have been easy to revamp the pre-war glory of the German might. Over three million men were killed at the front. At home, over a million died of starvation and destitution during four hard winters. The country would have to be rebuilt and it was going to be costly. Since all the money had been spent on the war effort, donations from other countries were inevitable. The German pride already hurt because of loosing the war, was thus wounded again, having to admit that it could no longer take care of its own. Those convinced that Germany should have been victorious were looking for a reason for the loss of the war. Soon the blame game started.

Living in a bankrupt country that depended on handouts from the rest of the world in the form of payments of reparations, the German people's will was broken. All around them they saw destruction, suffering, severe lack of food and medical care, and the grief from the loss of family members and friends. Among the numb masses left to mourn the dead and try to survive, there was a hard core of nationalists who not only firmly believed in the superiority of Germany, but who also used their words to kindle the dying, fiery spirit of people and country. Heralding the sinister belief that regardless of what the country was going through, the Germans had fought a just war and the veterans were the real heroes. This band of nationalist revisionists slowly created a movement that took several months to get a following. Most Germans didn't see it that way. There were other priorities, and frankly they didn't believe that playing the blame game would make their lives any easier. However, a group around the deposed army chief Drexler, often named those that were to be blamed: the Jews.

Rewriting all the causes that led to the defeat and humiliation of Germany proved difficult because it was based on lies. Granted, the core of the new movement could not dispute the fact that over ten thousand Jewish men had lost their lives fighting for the Kaiser on the battlegrounds in Europe, the fact that many Jews survived was now used against them. They became the traitors and the cause for the surrender of their beloved *Vaterland*.

It was with a lot of anger and hate that Helmut Drexler stopped with four other veterans on the Unterrathstrasse in Düsseldorf that morning. He knew that several Jews who served in the army lived on this street. His tactics were always the same; hand out pamphlets to people walking down the street while keeping an eye out for Jewish signs near the entrance of homes. The pamphlets, he reasoned, were needed to convince bystanders that he and his team had justification for carrying out small raids. In big bold letters the accusation jumped off the page: *Now We Know For Sure! The Jews Betrayed The Kaiser*. It then went into more detail about how the Jews were responsible for the sinking of the Lusitania. People should not associate with traitors. At the bottom was a single line that justified the raids. The Jews needed to pay! There were no names on the pamphlets, nor was the content claimed by any organization, which protected the nationalists in case the police showed up. However, no authoritative force had shown up during the two previous incidents, and Drexler was sure that several policemen across Germany actually supported their cause and reasoning as outlined in the pamphlets.

With quasi impunity the men proceeded to stir the anger of the passersby. As luck would have it, once again, there was an immediate source of assistance. A mailman wearing a dark and dirty, grey overcoat pulled Drexler aside and pointed at an off-white stucco home with wood beams above the doors and windows. This was one of the very few houses that had remained undamaged during the war, another sign to Drexler that the people who owned the house had collaborated with the enemy. He nodded and called to his men. They approached the front door of the home and noticed a porcelain sign with Hebrew lettering on it. One of the men immediately ripped the *shalom* sign off the doorpost and smashed it on the cobble stones in front of the house while Drexler beat his fist on the door.

A white bearded man opened the door. Peering over his small reading glasses with wide opened eyes, he looked at Drexler.

"What is the meaning of all the noise?" he asked.

"Out of my way old man," Drexler said, pushing the man aside.

Pointing at two of his men he continued, "Hold him here while we get restitution."

Drexler and three other men entered the house as the old man protested.

"Who gave you the right to come into my house?"

Drexler shrugged his shoulders as one of the men outside showed the old man the pamphlet. The old man stared at it in total disbelief.

"This is a lie! We fought for this country as all Germans did."

Drexler's man laughed as he turned to the other one.

"They fought all right. Against us, is what I heard."

"My son even fought against Jews from other countries! That's how loyal he was. You're spreading lies about us."

The men outside didn't bother to reply any further. While inside the house, glass was being broken, another car pulled up. Just as a young man got out of the car, one of Drexler's men came running out with a golden menorah, several silver cups and a few spoons. He dumped everything into their car and ran back into the house. The young man pushed the man holding the old man away.

"What are you doing here? Leave my father alone."

Although there was some initial shoving and pushing, the fight erupted in earnest when Drexler's men started throwing their fists into the old man and his son. Several bystanders had gathered and nobody moved a finger or said a thing. They looked at the spectacle more with embarrassment than with outrage. The old man's glasses were knocked off, and one of the men crushed them using his heel to smash them into mere glass shards. The fight got Drexler's attention. He came running out with a few paintings. Now on the ground, the old man saw what was happening and he cried out.

"No, not the paintings! They are worthless to you! Please leave them here!" he begged while trying to get up.

His son tried to get up as well, but a few hard kicks to his ribs had him curled up on the ground again. Drexler called out for his men inside who quickly brought out porcelain and crystal vases and smashed them in front of the house. They took off in their cars with the loot in the trunks.

The old man was helped up by a bystander while the son slowly got up by himself. One of the neighbors motioned for the onlookers to get lost and they scurried away from the scene. He then turned to the two injured men in the door opening.

"We are facing troubling times. Tell your congregation to leave this country. It will only get worse."

CHAPTER 6

Unterbilk
Monday afternoon, April 2, 1945

THE US 506TH Parachute Infantry Regiment had moved a few days before into what was called the Ruhr Pocket in the western part of Germany. The entire area had been bombed successfully by the allied forces in the months and weeks before, and the heavily industrialized engine of Germany was in ruins. Although few German pockets of resistance were left, Field Marshal Montgomery wanted to make sure Himmler's forces had not retreated back to the area. The Regiment stayed near the Rhine in the small village of Unterbilk.

The Regiment had initially been sent from the Alsace region to Mourmelon, France, where the entire 101st Airborne Division, stationed at Fort Bragg, NC, was the first division ever to be bestowed with the Distinguished Unit Citation Award by General Eisenhower. He honored their bravery and the division's successful stand at the battle of the Bulge in Belgium. Now, they had one final mission: complete a mop-up operation in the area before heading out toward Berchtesgaden, Hitler's Eagle's Nest.

Bill Thornton was part of a patrol group that concluded the final sweep of the southern suburbs of Düsseldorf. Although they knew that several people were hiding in bomb shelters, most had returned to their homes if they were still standing. Driving by one of the wider avenues, he spotted a curtain being moved on the lower floor of a house. He yelled to the driver of the jeep to halt. He jumped out, rifle in his hand.

"Hey Bill," the driver yelled. "Need any help?"

Bill didn't even turn around. He was sure of himself and waved off the suggestion. He kicked his boot against the door and it opened easily. He threw his cigarette on the ground, adjusted his helmet and entered, running from the narrow entrance hall to his right, toward the room where he assumed the curtain had been disturbed. The door was ajar so he pushed it open a little more with his rifle. He saw an empty sofa and a few foot lockers against the opposing wall. He heard the shot almost simultaneously with the breaking of a hallway mirror behind him.

"What the . . ." is all he could utter.

He was pissed that someone had taken a shot at him. He pushed with his foot against the door to open it all the way and saw that it had a bullet hole in it. He carefully looked around the doorpost into the room. In the corner he saw a young boy, about ten years old, fiddling with a gun. Realizing the child was not about to shoot again as he tried to figure out the weapon, Bill burst in and pointed his rifle at the boy's head. Immediately the young boy dropped the weapon and raised his arms. Bill looked around but could not spot anyone else, nor did he hear any other noises coming from inside the house.

"*Raus! Mach' schnell!*" he yelled at the boy, who disappeared toward the back of the house immediately.

Bill looked at all the foot lockers and crates stacked in the room. Almost sure that he had found a large stash of weapons, he used the butt of his rifle to knock off the lock of one of the crates. Giving his surroundings another quick look he opened the lid of the crate. Inside he saw burlap packed items. Holding his rifle pointed at the door to the back room, he pushed the burlap away from one item. All he saw was a frame.

"What do we have here?" he murmured.

With his free hand he pulled more away and saw that the item was a painting. He went to another crate, busting the lock. There was another set of burlap wrappings. He went to the footlockers and again he discovered nothing but paintings. He went back to the first crate and picked up the partially unwrapped painting, squeezed it under his arm and walked out backward pointing the rifle firmly in front of him. Once outside he turned around when the driver in the jeep noticed him.

"What took you so long, Thornton? We're done here."

Bill ran to the jeep as it was starting to move. He handed the painting to another soldier.

"What've you got here Bill?"

"A present from the owner. He was desperate to part with it."

"We thought for a second there you got hit, but through the window we saw you standing there."

"Nope, just a kid playing with a gun."

"So, what's in this thing?"

"A painting. It'll hang nicely in my house in Brooklyn."

"You're crazy."

"It's my reward for a crazy war."

The jeep sped away and Bill held on tight to the painting.

CHAPTER 7

Brooklyn, New York
Monday morning, June 18, 1945

THE HOUSES ON Sharon Street facing the park cast shadows over the road and the opposite sidewalk. There was very little going on besides the milkman putting fresh bottles out in corroded aluminum holders after taking out the empty ones. Leaving his delivery car running at every stop, he quickly made his way to the end of the street. Nobody else was outside. Presumably the end of war celebrations tired everyone out. People were resting inside perhaps or, those who had a job, were in the city or at one of the energy plants near the borough. Children were in school and the playground in the park looked deserted. It hadn't been painted since the thirties and grey ropes on the swings looked like they needed replacement before summer vacation when their strength and endurance would be tested as children pumped higher and higher.

Slowly, a canvas covered army truck pulled around the corner, the driver looking intently at the house numbers above the doors. In the back of the truck, Bill Thornton was gathering his duffel bag, hat, jacket and the wrapped painting. Every time during the past two months, when someone had asked him what he had in the burlap bag and how he got it, he answered the same way: the painting was a gift from a German family and it probably wasn't worth anything. Pressed as to why a German family would give him such a gift, he replied that he had saved someone's life. Of course in his own mind, the saving of a life was akin to not having taken one when he had the initial instinct to shoot the boy in that house in Düsseldorf. When he thought about it later, he knew that, if it had been an adult taking a shot at him with that German Luger, he would have killed that person, man or woman, without hesitation. The child had been more frightened than brave and he was lucky he was still alive. If he had been able to reload the gun, who knows how the war would have ended for the boy or himself.

Looking out from the back of the truck where the tarp was tied to the side, Bill saw familiar surroundings. Sharon Street was not very long, and when he saw the first set of houses with the large front porches and brick steps, he knew he was home.

"Okay guys, this is my stop."

The others shook his hand and patted him on the back.

Bill stood up and put on his jacket. He adjusted the cap on his head and saluted his fellow soldiers. The driver stopped the truck and yelled Bill's name through the small opening separating the cab from the back. Bill jumped out and reached for his bag and the painting. He gave the all clear by hitting on the back side of the truck, and the driver took off again.

He walked up the steps of the two story row house and pulled a little lever next to the small black sign with white lettering for his last name and the house number. He heard a bell far away followed by a door opening and slamming shut again. He was home.

Part II

REDUX

[Redux: Brought back; returned. Used postpositively]

CHAPTER 8

Saturday Morning

TOM ARDENS RAN a small art store in Queens and had made a mess of things. His business sense was limited to buying cheap and selling at the highest possible price. In itself, not a bad credo, but in his case, it had recently taken a wrong turn. Sitting at a small office desk in a corner of his store, Tom was contemplating the sale of a statue he knew was stolen. After a few small shaky dealings in the past, he had moved to an area of the business from which honest dealers stayed away. Of course, to himself, he could justify his reasons why he had needed to change his way of doing business. He didn't share his situation or manner of business with anyone especially when it came to his finances. His profits had declined and the bank loan would soon come due. To keep the store open, he had no other choice than to charge more and more for less valuable or illegal items. He figured that as long as customers didn't ask probing questions and kept paying his prices, he assumed he was going to be all right.

Running his right hand through his long, dirty blond hair, he looked at the pieces in the store as if mentally running an inventory. He put his sunglasses on his head, turned to his right and looked up and down a small bookcase of various art books. They served mostly as references when he had to look up a unique item, but, to be sure, each book was for sale. The older the book, the more he charged. He knew many people used the Internet to search for information on art pieces, but he was convinced that like him, a good many still wanted to look through a book. To Tom, a writer who was published was still more believable than an exposé by some art dealer on a web site, or God forbid, an art dealer with his or her own blog. On a small table, a stack of magazines sat next to a vase, a small painting on a small easel and a sword. Like everything in his store, these items had handwritten tags on them, dangling from white string. The descriptions on the labels might or might not include a specific year. He wanted to keep his options open. Lately, however, he had been revising the tags and things got suddenly older, some by many years.

Besides the plethora of display tables and a wall hung with several paintings, he also had a display window which showed some of his more attractive items. The Babylonian statue that was over 3,000 years old attracted many people into the store. It represented the bust of a Babylonian King with a small tiara, sharp facial features and a rectangular braided beard. Even though it was only about a foot tall, the chiseled cuneiform text below the beard was very clear. Next to the statue, Tom had a small painting on display. It rested on an easel and he hoped to sell the painting depicting a landscape any day. Various books and documents were offered in the window as well, but nothing ever had a price on the tag. The price for each item was kept on an index card in his desk drawer.

Leaning back in his chair, Tom rubbed his unshaven chin. The light growth on his tanned face looked like shining fuzz as the mid-morning sun brightened the room. On his desk lay a folded newspaper with the ad section on top. With a blue marker he had circled an announcement of the sale of the contents of a house in the area. He checked his watch and got up. He walked toward a small mirror hanging near the outside door and adjusted the collar of his light mauve tailored shirt of which the two top buttons were undone. He grabbed his dark blue, leather jacket from the back of a chair and as he retrieved his keys, the phone rang. He walked back to his desk and picked up the receiver:

"Arden Arts."

"Yes, I was walking by your store yesterday and saw what looked like a Ming vase. How much are you asking for it?" the caller asked.

Tom put his jacket back down and sat on the edge of the desk.

"It sells for sixty thousand."

Not only did he know that it wasn't the price on his index card, it wasn't a Ming vase. The customer didn't know that, and, as far as Tom was concerned, would never find out.

"That's quite pricey," the caller replied.

"Yeah, no kidding right? They're expensive suckers," Tom chuckled.

"Do you have any papers on it?"

"It's a genuine early Ming and it's expensive. I have the papers right here. It's well worth the sixty thousand."

"I'd like to come see it and check it out in more detail. How about next Tuesday?"

"That's fine. I'll see you on Tuesday then," Tom said and put the receiver down.

That type of call was exactly what he needed, but first he would have to fix the paperwork. He opened his desk drawer, took a folder that was lying on top of everything and put it on his desk. Looking into the drawer he paused for a few moments, staring at a small framed picture of a young man in uniform. A small black ribbon behind the glass covered the bottom. On it, in gold lettering, the name *Ron Arden* was printed. Pushing it slightly to the side, he took a piece of paper that he was after, and closed the drawer. The paper had Chinese and English written on it, and while he hadn't looked at the document in a while, he smiled when he saw that the line for the description was not filled in yet. Since this was his only official Chinese document, he carefully put the paper down on his desk and started the forgery. He took a fountain pen and on the empty line he slowly wrote the words *Tianshun Ming*. Satisfied that his writing matched the other handwritings onto the document with the Chinese characters also in black ink, he stood up and blew on the paper making sure the ink dried. He walked over to the vase and checked the tag. Four months ago, he had been excited when he bought the vase in a pawn shop in Queens. He had found out that it was a valuable vase from the Late Qing Dynasty and had put that on the tag. Now that he had a potential buyer, he ripped that tag off. He'd put a new one on as soon as he returned from the tag sale.

He picked up his jacket again when the door opened and a tall well-groomed man walked in. Tom turned around.

"Morning. How can I help you?"

The man stuck out his hand to shake Tom's. "Good morning. Are you the owner?"

"Yes, can I help you?"

The man moved toward the display window.

"I saw that small painting through the window. It's intriguing. What can you tell me about it?"

"It's a Jeffrey Oldens from 1922," Tom offered.

"I see . . . How much are you asking for it?

Tom grabbed the stack of index cards on his desk. "I have it here, just a second. Ah, here we go. That one is $3,900."

"Can I take a closer look?"

"No problem," Tom said as he handed him the painting.

The man took it with both hands and looked intently at the landscape in the painting. He took off his glasses to study a particular detail closer. He sighed when he lowered it and handed it back to Tom.

"I think it's beyond my budget. I need to think about it."

"Sure," Tom smiled. "It's well worth the price compared to some of his other works and, what's more important, very little of his work is left for sale, and I'm sure you understand all about demand."

"I do. Thanks. Maybe I'll stop by on Monday."

"I'll be here," Tom answered. "I usually close at 5:30 p.m."

"Fine, I may come by. I'll see you."

As the man left, Tom picked up the painting and studied it himself. There was nothing in the landscape that stood out or reminded him of anything. He shrugged his shoulders, put it back on the easel and walked to the small storage room at the back of the store. As he opened a box, again the door opened and he hurried back to the front.

Isabelle had closed the door and was already standing near Tom's desk when he walked in. She was wearing a bright yellow short sleeve top, tucked into stylish blue jeans with paisley forms stitched on the back pockets. She didn't have a lot of makeup on and her hazel eyes seemed to smile constantly. She had short black hair and long dangling earrings with a small yellow stone in them. Over her shoulder she wore a small blue purse and she was resting her left hand on the top.

"Hi, hiding in there again?" she said, stretching her upper body to steal a kiss from Tom.

"Hey sweetie, what brings you in here this morning?"

"Nothing special really. I just wanted to wish you good luck today in your search for treasure," she said, rolling the r's on the last word as if it was something mysterious and strange. "You haven't forgotten about that tag sale, have you?"

"No, I was about to leave. I'm late but I had a few potential customers. No sales."

"I have a feeling it's gonna be a good day for you. I'll keep my fingers crossed. Well, got to go into the office."

Isabelle gave Tom a peck on the cheek and turned toward the door.

"Working at the Metropolitan on a Saturday?"

"I need to catch up on some work. I'll see you around six tonight. Call me when you get back from the sale."

"I will. Hey, Izzy!"

"What?"

"Drive carefully."

"See ya," she said and walked out, letting the door close by itself.

Tom took his jacket, flung it over his left shoulder holding it by the loop inside the collar and took the newspaper from his desk. He stuck it under his left arm. He turned the sign on the door to "Will be back at 2 p.m." and turned off the main light. He took his keys and stole a quick peek in the small mirror on the wall, adjusted his hair and walked out, locking the door behind him.

It was a warm spring day and he debated for a second whether or not to leave his jacket in the office, but then pushed his key to unlock his pale blue Porsche Boxter parked in front of the office. Leaning into the car after he opened the passenger door, he was folding his jacket carefully on the seat when a man walked up to him and tapped his shoulder. The man had an unkempt appearance and wore an old brown suit that was at least a size too large.

"Hey, Tom!" the man said in a deep smoker's voice.

Tom was startled and looked around.

"Luke! Jeez man, you scared me."

"It's your guilty conscience." Luke practically coughed out the words while taking a cigarette out and lighting it.

"What's up?" Tom said, closing the door and walking around the car. He opened the driver's side door.

Luke followed him closely.

"You know that you're two months behind, right?" he said after taking a long drag, blowing smoke out with every word he spoke.

"I'll have the rent to you by next Thursday," Tom said, getting into his car.

Luke put his hand on the top of the door, preventing Tom from closing it, when, to the annoyance of Tom, he blew smoke right into the car.

"That's your last chance Tom. I have another renter who's ready to move in."

"Hey, listen. I told you I'd have it next week, alright? You're polluting my car by the way."

"Well, you heard me. I mean it," Luke said while slamming the door shut.

Tom started the car, revving the engine excessively.

"Asshole," he murmured and drove off.

CHAPTER 9

Later That Saturday Morning

TOM TURNED ONTO Sharon Street a little fast and had to slam on the brakes to avoid a parked car. Relieved his Porsche handled it well, he was also concerned about all the cars parked on both sides of the street. He wondered whether this was a special tag sale, and grew doubtful anything of value would be left. He quietly cursed himself for not showing up earlier. He drove on slowly until he saw the big *Assisted Moving* sign in front of the two story row house. There were a few people standing in the small driveway, lined up to go inside, a sign that it was really busy. Ignoring the *No Parking* sign in front of the garage, he carefully wedged his way between a brick wall and the people. Locking up his car, he noticed those in line staring at him. The hell with it, he thought. There's nowhere else to park. If someone asked him to move it he would. He put on his jacket and joined those in line.

The woman in front of him turned to him right away.

"Hi. Looking for something today?" she asked, looking him up and down, curious why a young, well dressed and good-looking man would be interested in an ordinary sale.

"Nothing special, I think most of the stuff will have been picked over." Tom smiled, relieved that she didn't give him grief about his parking.

"Not to worry young man. It's a tag sale and people can bid on things, so sometimes it's better coming a little later. You can always bid higher," she said. Several people were leaving, carrying cardboard boxes with stuff.

"Yeah, I guess so," he answered absently while looking at what people were carting off. Nothing of value, he concluded.

He turned back to the woman, but the line was already being allowed inside.

There was a musty smell in the house, the smell of worn out carpet, dusty curtains and old people. It took a while to move through the first room, an old fashioned sitting or formal room, with two couches and two chairs pushed against the walls. Someone had moved the coffee table over to the door, freeing up the space in the middle so that buyers could look around at the paintings, clearly prints, a few lampshades and a pile of books. Nothing here, he figured and moved to the family room which had been connected to the kitchen by removing a wall. The family's entire collection of porcelain, old electronic gadgets and a TV were on display here. He stopped briefly to look at a laptop. On the keyboard a small sticker warned the buyer that the laptop was a slow dog and that it had a bad virus. Tom shook his head and walked over to a table of silver items which had been polished for the occasion. Nothing stood out. At another table he picked up a few small figurines, a chipped Lladro, and several instrumental Hummels. He spotted a deep platter that looked like a Delft blue. He immediately checked the bottom and found he was right. The mark was clear. He ran his hand along the entire rim, turning it up and down all over for a visual inspection. It was in good shape, actually perfect shape, he thought. They wanted fifty dollars for it, which meant not much of a margin for him. He put it down, and on the tag filled in a bid of twenty, added his telephone number, and moved on.

Kitchen areas usually were a waste of time for Tom at these sales and a quick glance was sufficient for him to confirm this, so he moved upstairs. He shrugged when he saw the staircase lined with pictures and paintings, all products of amateurs. On the landing he noticed a Japanese print. Upon closer inspection, he found a tiny sewn on label that placed its manufacturer in Hong Kong. Resigned to the fact that besides the Delft platter he was not going to find anything here, he quickly moved through the three bedrooms which were littered with linens, puzzles, lamps and books. Nothing piqued his interest and he skipped the bathroom altogether.

At the bottom of the stairs, an older man stopped Tom.

"Hi, any electronics upstairs?"

"No, didn't see any," Tom replied.

"Thanks, you're saving me a trip up there. With these knees it's a chore, you know."

"I get you," Tom said, ready to move along.

"Hey, do you play piano by any chance? You look like a musician," the man said.

Tom chuckled. "A musician, me? No, I'm an art dealer. Why do you ask?"

"I just thought . . . There's a beautiful piano in that den over there," the man said.

"Oh, well, thanks. I'll check it out," Tom replied and walked over to the den, having missed it earlier.

It was never easy for him to get his bearings in a stranger's house. In the future he might consider asking for a floor plan, he thought, while entering the den. At least he wouldn't skip any rooms by mistake. The den was almost completely filled with a small, white lacquered concert piano. It was a butterfly grand, with its two lids unfolded like wings, ready to carry the music up into the air, except that no one was playing. The only noise was the loud hum of people talking in the other rooms. The tag said it was a 1927 Wurlitzer and sold for two thousand. It was probably worth a lot more, but not of interest to him. He looked up and saw two paintings hanging on the walls. One was a landscape and the other a portrait of an old man with a long white beard. The landscape was painted in bright colors, using wide brushstrokes and a lot of dabbed multi-colored areas. It was nicely done, but too much like what he had seen on TV where the teacher showed the technique in everything he painted, from trees to rooftops. Tom didn't recognize the artist's name. As light as the first painting was, the second one had a somber, dark look. Tom looked for a light shining on the painting, but soon realized that the artist had painted it in such a way that the light emanated from an unknown source, allowing the viewer to see the detail of the old man's face. In his lap he was holding an infant that looked to be no more than a month old, but with the facial features of a one year old. Hard to figure, Tom thought. He stepped back and looked at it again from inside the doorway. The whole composition reminded him of something, but he couldn't put his finger on it. He knew one thing for sure; if this was as old as he thought it was, he'd buy it.

As he walked back inside the den, a voice interrupted his thoughts.

"Hi, are you interested in the paintings?" a woman asked.

Tom turned around and saw a woman, perhaps in her fifties. She wore a company name tag.

"Elena, is it? Can you tell me something about these paintings?

"Oh no, I don't know anything. The owner has already moved to an assisted living facility," she said with a smile.

"Didn't he or she make an inventory list or something?"

"I don't know sir. Let me check to see whether Chris, her daughter, is still here."

While the woman walked away, Tom took the painting off the wall and looked intently at the paint. He was still holding it when another woman walked up to him.

"Good morning, you must be Chris. I'm Tom," he said.

"Hi, Tom, is that the painting you were asking about?"

"Yes, there's no name on it. Do you know where it comes from or how old it is?" Tom asked. He didn't really expect an answer because at many other tag or estate sales, owners seldom knew the painter or how old it was.

"My dad bought some paintings at furniture stores, but I think he brought that one back from overseas. He loved that painting. It may be a hundred years old, I have no clue."

"I don't see any signature or name on it. Did he know who painted it?"

"No, my dad liked the anonymity of things. He pretended all those were painted by unknown masters; at least that's what he told us. Sorry, I can't help you."

"No problem, I just wonder what this portrays."

Chris smiled, recalling her father's attachment to the painting.

"Dad called it 'Grandpa the babysitter.' I'm sure he invented it."

Tom took a closer look at the painting. He noticed tiny cracks and ran his finger gently along the painted seam of the old man's robe that showed muted brilliant colors covered by years of airborne dirt, but still reflecting the light contrasting the darkness of the surrounding room.

It gave the old man a distinct, physical presence. The baby on the old man's lap was wrapped in linens and appeared wide awake.

"So, this one he bought overseas, right?"

"Actually, I remember him telling us that it was a gift from a German."

"Fascinating! Why do you want to sell it?"

"Mom doesn't want any of it and we're not that big on art. We also don't think they're worth that much."

Tom looked at the tag dangling from the bottom of the frame.

"One hundred and fifty huh . . . Will you take one hundred?"

"You'll need to speak to Elena. She's with Assisted Moving. Anyway, I've got to go. Good luck."

The woman left and Tom spotted Elena in the hallway. He walked over to her with the painting in his hands.

"Elena, I think I want to buy this one." Tom said walking up to her.

The woman looked at the tag.

"One fifty. You can go to our checkout in the garage."

"Can we settle on one hundred?"

"You can leave a bid for that much. If you want it now, it's one fifty," she said smiling, and added "Excuse me, I'm needed upstairs."

Tom studied the painting again and got a good feeling about it. He stared at nothing particular on the ceiling, trying to think of where he had seen something like that. He knew he wanted it but didn't know why it intrigued him so much. He worked his way to the garage and while standing in line, he checked his pockets and counted the bills in his pocket, realizing he didn't have enough. He walked up to the person at the small cash register.

"Can I pay by check?" he asked, putting the painting on the table.

"Sure, make it out to *Assisted Moving*. Let's see," she said, inspecting the tab. "That'll be one hundred and fifty."

Tom grabbed a single check from inside his jacket pocket, and sighed. He crossed out *Rent* on the memo line, wrote *Painting* and filled in the rest of the check. He stuffed the receipt in his pocket and walked out, taking a deep breath of fresh air. He felt like a little boy who just won first prize, but didn't yet know what to do with it.

CHAPTER 10

Saturday Noon

TOM WAS RESTING his hands on his desk. He was hanging over the painting, studying it carefully. He still had on his jacket. His ride home had heightened his excitement. He'd get good money for this he figured, because he was sure it was older than the lady had thought. The tiny fractured lines in the paint, the quality of the brushstrokes, and the detail in the old man's face and hands were hopeful signs. The slightly damaged frame and the darkness were not so good. Everything in the background was so dark he couldn't see anything on the walls, if there was anything painted there at all.

He took a step back from his desk, took off his jacket, selected a few books from the bookcase and sat down. He leafed through the volume on old etchings and engravings first, starting from the fifteenth century, working forward. Nothing looked like it, until he found a Dürer etching of St. Christopher. It was actually an engraving from 1521. The old man had the same beard, he looked left, but the child was on his shoulders. It did have the larger head, but he had seen that many times in paintings. He found a more detailed etching of what would later become a great masterwork, a depiction of St. Jerome, again an old man, but this time with his hand on a skull. Tom shook his head, comparing the facial features to the work lying on his desk. Further searching in the book did not yield anything that looked like the old man. He put the first book down and took another one on Flemish and Dutch artists and their works, hoping he would find a clue in it. He kept looking for etchings because often they evolved in several paintings that showed the study and evolution of paintings and the painter. He kept looking page after page for something similar to his painting, especially those with an old man and a child in it.

He was near the end of the book when he found what he was looking for; a painting by Rembrandt. Tom's heart skipped a beat. He looked closer at his painting and noticed a few similarities: the mustache was curled the same way, distinguishing it intricately from the white beard on the cheek, the body was turned to the left the same way and the baby was also in his arms. It was painted in 1652 and belonged to The Hermitage in St Petersburg. Tom noticed that the light was used to accent the left side of the man's face. However, in the painting with the baby, the man's head was turned more to the left and there were some differences in the eyes and forehead. Had somebody copied a Rembrandt and given it his own interpretation, or was it done by one of his students?

Tom was suddenly overwhelmed by the possibilities. He was tempted to call Izzy but decided against it. Instead he stood up and for some reason locked the door to his store. He felt chilled to the bone. He hadn't eating anything for lunch and he was nervous.

"Christ, if this is a Rembrandt, I . . ."

He didn't finish his sentence. He didn't want his mind racing into the future. He had to make sure, because if it wasn't a Rembrandt the disappointment would be huge. He kept looking for old men but came up empty handed. He studied the painting again. It was hard to tell, but the clothing of the men in both paintings looked similar. It may have been red in the mystery painting, but he couldn't be sure. With a magnifying glass, Tom looked at the hands. His eyes widened in disbelief; they were exactly the same hands. No doubt about it.

From his bookcase he took a small book about Rembrandt. He knew it was only a primer with only a small selection of his oeuvre, but his answer may be right here he thought. When he was sure that his painting was not in the book, he looked at a number of pencil drawings by the old master. And then, there it was: an old man with a baby on his lap! Tom's heart skipped a beat. This time he fully succumbed to the suspense. It didn't matter that this sketch was a mirror image of the painting on his desk. He had bought a Rembrandt at that tag sale! He held his hands to his head.

"Holy shit, this can't be, can it?" he asked of himself out loud.

He grabbed the magnifying glass again and started looking intently for a signature. He knew Rembrandt used many variations of his name from his initials to his full name. His search turned up nothing at all.

"Perhaps a fake, after all . . ." he murmured.

He carefully looked at all possible places, especially the corners, but found nothing. Each corner was practically black and nothing else was painted on top of it. He turned the painting over but all he saw was the number 1945 written in red on the back of the frame. Studying the back, he noticed that some of the canvas was folded between the stretcher frame and the gilded frame. He took pliers and a screwdriver from his desk drawer and started wiggling the frame loose on one of the corners. He checked regularly to see if the front of the frame was getting damaged, but it looked okay, so he continued taking the glued frame apart. After he had two corners loose, the other sides came off easily. He immediately saw something was odd: extra canvas had been folded onto the stretcher frame and covered by the larger frame. That was never good, but in this case, Tom had a hunch. His heart raced a little faster, hoping he would find the reason why someone had done this. He took out some nails that held the fold against the stretcher frame and carefully unfolded the extra canvas. He talked out loud to himself.

"Okay, here we go. C'mon, c'mon, show me an *R* baby."

After three folds he clearly saw the top of the letter R in a painters palate form and quickly unfolded the rest. The name *Rembrandt* was as clear as day, even through the wrinkles.

"Yes! Yes! This is it! Oh man, the fucking real deal!" he yelled.

Tom was so excited he didn't know where to run first. He finally stood still in front of the canvas while he put his hand on his forehead.

"Oh baby. I've struck gold!"

He took his cell phone out of his jacket pocket and speed dialed Isabelle. There was no longer any doubt. He had a genuine Rembrandt in front of him, here in his store. Imagine, a masterpiece! Probably worth as much as . . . He did not finish his thought as Isabelle answered.

"Hello, Isabelle," she said.

"Izzy, you won't believe what I just bought! This is fucking crazy. I can't believe it. This could be the find of . . ."

"Tom, calm down. What do you have?" she asked, never having heard Tom stumble over his words like someone was chasing him.

"A Rembrandt!" he yelled.

"Hold on. Are you kidding me? Where did you find that? Wait, you're messing with me, right?"

"No, really, I bought this painting on a hunch at the tag sale and I'm sure it's real. The signature was hidden, but I recognized the painting from an earlier sketch Rembrandt made. I found it in one of my books."

"That's unbelievable, Tom. Hold it together, I'm leaving now. I'll be there in thirty minutes. Don't tell anyone else."

"I locked the store up. You have a key. Hurry before I pass out here."

CHAPTER 11

Saturday Afternoon

TOM BEAT ISABELLE to the door and opened it for her.

"I'm so excited. Let me see it!" Isabelle said, giving him a brief kiss on his lips.

Tom pointed to his desk.

"Right there, it took me a while to discover the signature."

"What have you done to it?" Isabelle asked as she ran to the desk.

"You mean the frame?"

"Well, yeah! You broke it. And look at the canvas. It looks like an accordion. What the hell, Tom?"

"No, wait. It's not what you think. The frame was damaged anyway and I wanted to find a name. This painting used to be larger. Look at the black on this side. Someone scaled the whole painting down after this side burned, and folded the remainder on a new stretcher frame."

Isabelle didn't answer right away. She looked intently at the painting and then at the etching in the book on the desk.

"It sure looks like the sketch," she said, "but I'm a bit skeptical."

"Why? That's Rembrandt's signature, isn't it?" he asked while both were still staring at the painting.

"We've got to be very careful with this Tom. I don't want to disappoint you, but this is not as simple as it seems."

"What are you saying?" Tom asked looking at her.

"First of all, it looks genuine and if I were to guess, I'd say it is real," she said picking up the magnifying glass.

"It's got to be. It came from Europe," Tom said.

"That in itself is not a guarantee," she said as she studied the painting closer. "On the other hand, this is an original."

She stood up and smiled.

"This is an old painting Tom. You may be right," she said, bending over again to study a particular detail on the old man's hand. "Of course, it will have to stand up to some scrutiny."

"Like what?"

"As excited as you are about this, you need to realize that there are forgeries out there and any skilled artist can paint from a sketch and it can be made to look about 400 years old."

"If it's a forgery, it would have been painted before 1945," Tom said, pointing to the date on the back of the frame. "I believe the owner's daughter said it was given to him by a German."

"Listen, even if it isn't a Rembrandt, but by one of his students, it's still worth a lot of money."

"Well that would still be good," Tom sulked.

"You know what? Monday morning when I get to work, I'll tell Dr. Amado. I'm sure he'll want to take a look at it. But please, don't get your hopes up Tom," she said slowly. "You know, there's a bit of research that we can do now, before you take it to him. I mean, if this is an existing painting, it must be known and I'm sure we can find out something."

"I can't wait. This is so fucking unbelievable," Tom said, getting excited again. He took a picture of the painting with his iPhone. "I'm going to get some books."

Isabelle inspected the painting while Tom went to the back room to get the books. With four books under his arm, he walked back to the storefront while quickly sending the picture to a friend with the subject line *Masterpiece for sale—call me.*

"What are you doing?" Isabelle asked.

"Letting Kevin know. He knows buyers from his job at Sotheby's and all."

"But you don't know yet whether this is a real Rembrandt. Wait until Monday and even then, I wouldn't want to advertise that you have a possible treasure here in your store."

"You're right. I'll text Kevin to hold it under wraps," Tom said, sending a short message.

"Let me get my laptop from the car. Let's do some research," Isabelle said, walking out of the store.

Tom sat at his desk with books all around the painting. He looked again in the book he had checked first and studied the etchings more.

This time he read a description of the mirror image of the painting in the text to the left of the etching.

"Hey Izzy, I think I know the name of the painting if the sketch is right. It's called *The Circumcision of Christ,*" he said as Isabelle walked back in.

"That's a good start. Remember that names of paintings sometimes change, so keep an open mind when you go through your books. I'm using my laptop."

"Books are faster," Tom smiled.

"We'll see who finds something first," she smiled back.

Isabelle sat down at one of the tables and started typing. She logged in at the employee portal on the Metropolitan's web site and started a search.

"So, we're looking at a rabbi, I guess, and he's holding a baby."

"If it's a rabbi he's not doing the cutting. The *mohel* does that. No, I think the rabbi is holding the baby boy ready and steady."

"I see . . . What are you looking up?" he asked watching her typing away.

"There's got to be something we can find out on the Internet, so I'm searching and . . . wait, here we go. Here is a reference to a Rembrandt painting that suddenly was no longer part of an estate in 1756. It was called The Circumcision . . ." Isabelle said all excited. She read on quickly and continued. "It was originally painted for Stadhouder Frederik Hendrik of Orange in 1646. That's promising, but I don't know what a Stadhouder is or where he's from."

Tom was listening and reading at the same time and stabbed his finger on a page in one of his art history books.

"Hold on, listen to this: *The Circumcision of Christ is the seventh painting by Rembrandt for the Stadhouder of the Netherlands who paid 2400 florins for it, a huge sum at the time.*"

"House of Orange, of course, that's Holland," Isabelle said, searching for the Stadhouder's information.

Tom took another book and started going through the index.

"There's got to be more to that painting than who commissioned it. I'm looking up what happened to it later."

"Meanwhile, I got the info on that Stadhouder Frederik Hendrik: Stadhouder is the title of the Dutch head of state. He is also referred to as the Prince. He collected plenty of art according to our Met web site," Isabelle said. "Anything more on its history?"

"Still looking," Tom said.

"Oh, look here. It was the wife of a descendant of this Frederik Hendrik who suddenly listed only six paintings after a restoration. Those are called the *Passion* paintings. Nothing's mentioned about *The Circumcision* anymore."

"And it ends up in Queens. What the hell happened to it for about two hundred and fifty years?" Tom wondered.

"Beats me, but with this information we at least know that such a painting existed," Isabelle said slowing down toward the end of the sentence as she looked intently at her screen.

"What'd you find?"

"I found that etching you too found in the book, but it was made in 1654. At least it said it was called *The Circumcision*, but something doesn't look right."

Tom got up and looked over her shoulder.

"No, that's not it," he said, taking his book and showing her a penciled drawing of just an old man and a baby.

"Well, let's see," she said, going back to the computer.

Tom waited and looked through the book. He didn't find the 1654 etching at all. Isabelle had more luck.

"Okay, here are etchings of 1626 and 1630. The first one looks a lot more like the painting you found."

"And that one is called *The Circumcision*, right?"

"Yes, and look here. Rembrandt painted no less than five paintings with circumcision as the subject."

"And this one is the only one missing."

"That's correct. The others are accounted for."

"Which will make it easy for Dr. Amado, right?"

"Yes and no. I hate to be he devil's advocate here, but if we can find the history of the painting in ten minutes, so can anyone else and there are some clever forgers out there. We've only got a sketch of something similar, not a picture of the real thing."

Tom closed the book and stared out of the window.

"I understand, but I'm still excited. It would be worth millions, right?"

"That's for sure, but Monday we should find out more. And, we'll do more research.

"Right! You know, Izzy, if this is indeed a Rembrandt, it would take care of all my problems.

CHAPTER 12

Monday Morning

THE DRIVE TO the Metropolitan Museum didn't take more than a half hour. To beat the traffic, Tom had left about nine thirty, so he was on time for his appointment with the famous Dr. Amado. He was actually lucky to find a parking spot on East 82nd Street, a two minute walk to the Met. He ran up the steps, carrying the large garbage bag. He was oblivious to the many people on the plaza, staring at him. He entered through one of the opened doors and saw Isabelle.

"They're waiting for you," she smiled, walking ahead of Tom.

"Sorry about the bag, I couldn't find anything else," he said.

"Don't worry, as long as you packed it carefully to protect the canvas."

Tom didn't answer and followed her past the waiting line and through security. Isabelle opened a side door with her electronic card, and they were in the offices of the Met. He had never been in here and was immediately impressed by the quiet. The noise in the foyer had seemed normal to him in such an environment, but here behind the walls, it seemed almost peaceful. Isabelle greeted a few people but did not bother to introduce Tom as they worked their way to one of the elevators.

They got off on the second floor and walked in a hallway to the side of the exhibition rooms. A locked door was opened by a security guard and they entered the inner sanctum of the offices. Isabelle stopped in front of a door with a sign that said *Restoration*.

"I'm keeping my fingers crossed," she whispered as she knocked and pushed the door open.

Inside the room, three men were standing by a large table that looked like a drafting table. It was slightly tilted from the back down to the front with a wooden slat at the bottom of the front side. They turned their heads and Isabelle walked up to a stately older man in his sixties. He had a sharp face, a somewhat large nose upon which small reading glasses sat. His hair was still mostly black, combed back and quite long at the neck. His designer suit was helping to hide a bit of a large belly and gave him an elegant look. Isabelle gently took his elbow and turned him toward Tom.

"Dr. Amado, this is Tom Ardens."

She added, "Tom, Dr. Amado is the head curator here. This is his team of experts."

Dr. Amado looked at Tom intently as if sizing him up. He knew he was Isabelle's boyfriend, so he was a bit curious.

"Nice to meet you Mr. Arden,"

Tom and Dr. Amado shook hands.

"Nice to meet you, sir," he said.

Dr. Amado introduced him to the other men.

"So, let's take a look at the painting you brought us," he said.

Tom put the garbage bag next to the tilted table and pulled out a piece of the gilded frame, then another, and another. All three men cringed when Tom finally raised the canvas on the feeble stretcher frame out of the bag. He had used Saran wrap to protect it.

"Careful with that, young man. If this is what you say it is, we need to treat this like a baby."

"A very valuable one, right?" Tom asked.

"Well, let's take a look at it first, Mr. Arden. Can I call you Tom?" Dr. Amado asked.

"Sure," Tom said, putting the frame on the table.

Dr. Amado turned to the other men, "Gentlemen?"

In unison, the three men bent over the canvas. They each had a magnifying glass. It became eerily quiet in the room and Tom looked at Isabelle, crossing his arms while Isabelle shrugged her shoulders. After a short while, the men looked at each other as if they were ready to give their opinion. Dr. Amado motioned his head to the canvas and they went back to studying it. Tom was biting his lip and Isabelle put her arm around his shoulders. He was obviously very nervous and it would have been devastating for him if their immediate verdict was negative.

Finally, Dr. Amado stood up straight and turned to Tom, taking a deep breath.

"This is an amazing piece. First let me say that it looks like an old painting, most likely 17th century."

"Great," Tom said with obvious relief in his voice.

"Of course," Dr. Amado concluded, "We cannot exclude that it is a brilliant Rembrandt forgery or something painted by one of his students. Having said that, of course, we will have to go through an authentication procedure."

"So, you think it is a Rembrandt?"

"It looks very much like it at first inspection, but we don't know this painting. Supposedly there is a copy of the original in Braunschweig, in Germany. I don't have a copy of it here, but from what I remember, it was a copy of the central figure, the old man I suppose, embellished with good-looking maidens in the background and some paraphernalia that Rembrandt couldn't have painted in his time. So, not much to go on."

"Isabelle and I checked it out and we're sure it was a painting that was supposedly lost. I have the history here," Tom said, giving Dr. Amado a manila folder with a few sheets of paper in it.

"We will check this out, thank you."

"So, how long will this authentication process take, and what really happens?" Tom asked.

Dr. Amado was a true scientist who was keen on prefacing his answer with basic facts on which the answer was built.

"You must realize that first there are many variables involved in the making of a work of art. Consider all the elements used in creating a painting: canvas, pencil marks, paint pigments and oils, the wood of the frame, and so on. Then there is the style, or perhaps the evolving style of the painter with signature brushstrokes, a special eye for detail, the presentation of skin, the grasp of the underlying skeletal assumption and so much more."

Tom was getting a little impatient and shifted on his feet from side to side. Isabelle saw that Tom was going to say something that might irritate Dr. Amado and quickly intervened.

"So, Dr. Amado, how will you go about examining this particular painting?"

"Glad you asked, Isabelle. In this case, we will examine the paint composition, the age and origin of the ingredients. We have a lot of paint to work within the part that was folded."

Tom nodded. "Okay, I get that, but will you then be sure?"

Dr. Amado smiled and continued.

"As I was about to say, then the painting has to be evaluated by a Dutch expert. It will be days before he gets here, so you will have to be patient."

"But you have a pretty good idea about it being a Rembrandt, right?"

Dr. Amado looked at his staff members but none replied or showed agreement.

"As I said, Tom, it looks like it, but . . ."

"Okay, that's good enough for me. How do we sell it?"

"Once we have the utmost certainty, and, equally important, once we can verify that there is no outstanding claim on it, you'll have several options."

"Well, I bought it and I have the receipt to prove it. That would make it mine, right? So, what is the fastest option?"

Isabelle was getting annoyed with Tom. She had warned him over the weekend not to hammer at selling the painting because that was not Dr. Amado's concern. He was a curator whose first responsibility was the protection and conservation of quality artwork. She turned to Tom.

"Tom, why don't we discuss this later? We can leave Dr. Amado and his team to do their work."

"Alright, I guess . . ." Tom said reluctantly. He turned back to Dr. Amado.

"I assume you'll call me as soon as you have an answer?"

Dr. Amado gently smiled.

"You can count on it. Now, we'd like to get back to our work," he said as he shook hands with Tom.

CHAPTER 13

Monday Noon

TOM HAD PICKED up lunch from McDonald's on the way in to the office. He wasn't really sure how he felt after his meeting at the Met. On the one hand, he was excited about the fact that Dr. Amado and his team had not immediately dismissed the painting as being something else. As a matter of fact, he was convinced that they were sure that it was a Rembrandt, a heavily damaged one, but still a Rembrandt. On the other hand, he had that weird feeling that they were not telling him everything. The way Dr. Amado had stressed how important it was to have the painting authenticated using all those elements, made him have just enough doubt to worry. But they had said it was from the 17th century, so it was old and worth money. That gave Tom some peace of mind. While waiting in the drive-thru, he had wondered what that so-called Dutch expert was going to do. Actually, that was a good thing because it meant that they really thought it was a Rembrandt, so this guy must be an authority on Rembrandt's work.

The drive back from downtown, including his stop for food, had taken over an hour. Tom put the salad on his desk and got a small bottle of water from the back room. As he sat down, he opened the plastic container with the salad in it, and made a call.

"Hey Kevin! What's up man?" he asked, taking the first forkful of salad.

"Not much," Kevin said sleepily.

Tom swallowed quickly.

"I'm just curious. Did you get the picture I sent you Saturday?"

"I did. What was that about?"

"That picture I sent you is a painting. I just got back from the Met and their head curator says it's a Rembrandt. Can you fucking believe it?"

"Wow, that's amazing!" Kevin said, more awake now. "A Rembrandt, huh? So, what do you want to do with it?"

"What do you think? It'll take a few days to have it authenticated and then I want to sell it as soon as possible. Interested?"

"Yeah, I'm sure we can handle it. Man, if you're right, you'll make a bundle. Why don't I . . ." he started, but Tom wasn't listening any more. He was distracted by a customer walking into his store. The man wore blue slacks, a white shirt and a tan sport jacket. He had gray hair that was neatly combed back. His eyes were constantly scanning and Tom could tell that he had the cough of a smoker.

The man started to look at a book. Tom got the feeling he was actually trying to listen intently to his conversation with Kevin.

Tom listened to Kevin and answered.

"Of course, I can come in this afternoon and meet with your boss." He lowered his voice a little and continued, "At least we can discuss selling it. It's got to be worth a few mil. What do you say?"

"I'll talk to him and text you back."

"I can be there by two. Thanks, buddy," Tom said, hanging up the phone, getting up to talk to his customer.

"Can I help you?"

"Yes, uh, remember me? I bought that Civil War document about four months ago. It was an appointment letter of my great grandfather to the rank of general. Remember? My name is Marco Vincente."

Tom took a second or two to answer.

"Oh yeah, I do remember. What's up?"

"Well, a funny thing happened the other day. I showed that document to a cousin of mine and he says he has the same thing. So, we go to his house and sure enough, my unique piece has a twin. What do you think of that?" Marco said, raising his voice as he spoke.

Tom felt threatened right away. A dissatisfied customer who came back was not an ideal situation. They usually wanted something and it was not another piece of art. He took a deep breath and stayed calm.

"It's odd, I guess. Now, letters did get copied," Tom explained, "but what are the chances that there was a copy, and that it survived, and was also sold. Quite coincidental. That's history for you," he smiled at the man and went back to his desk.

"Oh, I know, history is fascinating, but he also showed me his receipt. He paid about a quarter of what I paid. You overcharged me!"

Tom realized he had been right. Trouble right here, he thought, and this didn't look like an easy customer. Nevertheless, he'd try to use all the tricks in the book.

"I sell everything at fair market value, sir."

"Well, the way I see it, I'm out an extra fifteen hundred dollars and that would come in handy right now, you know?"

"Maybe, but all sales are final. There's nothing I can do for you."

Tom expected the man to get really pissed, but he didn't. Marco Vincente was as calm as could be. He sat down in a chair next to Tom's desk and got comfortable.

"Let's say you don't have the money right now. Fine. The least you could do is to admit that you overcharged me and that you would make this right if you had the money."

"Listen, even if I had the money, I don't revisit a closed deal. Now, if you'll excuse me, Mr. Vicente," he said walking toward the door, opening it slightly.

"Hold on there buddy. I'm not going anywhere yet. You're a professional art dealer, right?"

"Of course I am," Tom said, closing the door and crossing his arms.

"Then you should have a better idea of what something is worth. Is that how you treat all your customers?"

"Sir, I run a respectable business. Now, have a good day."

Tom walked over and sat down at his desk and gestured toward the door. He was not going to open it a second time for this guy. Marco, on the other hand, stayed put, leaning forward toward Tom.

"It sounds to me like you may come into some money. I'm sure fifteen hundred dollars will be a drop in the bucket."

"As I said, a deal is a deal. I work hard to make this business successful."

Marco sat back.

"I see," he said and pointed with his thumb over his shoulder toward the outside of the store. He continued: "That's your car outside, the blue one, right?"

Tom had been resolute and firm so far and was not giving an inch, as he had done many times. Most customers would take the hint and leave. Of course, he would never see them again, but he was not interested in hanging on to difficult customers. This man Marco was getting a little persistent in hanging around.

"Yeah. Why do you ask?"

"Your registration has expired," Marco replied.

"What the hell does that have to do with anything?" Tom asked, no longer being polite.

"You do remember that I was a detective, right? I may be retired, but I notice these things. If a cop was to check it out, would he find your insurance lapsed as well?" he grinned.

Tom leaned back in his chair. "What are you getting at?"

"Just saying, just saying. I visit the station around here often, and I know a few fellows that haven't reached their quota yet this month."

"You wouldn't!" Tom said loudly.

"Well, let's say that you need money badly to pay for all of this and a few minutes ago when you were on the phone it sounded to me like your ship may have come in."

"I work on big deals every day. Look, I need to get something ready for a customer. Have a good day."

"All right," Marco said and stood up, pushing the chair back to the desk. He walked to the door. Before opening it he took one of Tom's business cards from a holder and pretended to study it for a while. He then turned around.

"Arden . . . You're Ron Arden's son right, he was from Levittown?"

Tom looked up, a little startled. How did this man know that? Christ, he had never even met his own father, and here was a guy, practically a stranger, making that connection.

"Yes. Did you know him?"

"We were together in 'Nam."

Tom knew his father's story, of course, but this guy had figured out exactly who he was. Why didn't he speak up when he bought the damn document, he thought. It's not like he could have missed the name Arden on the store window. Tom had no clue as to what this man was up to. He decided to keep this short.

"I see," he said.

"So, you're Ron's son."

"I never knew my dad."

"I know."

"Well, anyway, sorry I couldn't help you."

Marco however, was determined to stay a while longer, and continued as if he hadn't gotten the hint to leave.

"I knew him for about two years."

Tom had no idea how to terminate this conversation. He wanted the guy to leave because all he was going to do was ask for his money back, but he also had a chance to learn something about his dad. His mother had never shared everything with him.

"My mother told me that he came home in a box with the last troops," Tom said in a matter of fact way.

"I was there at Saigon's *Tan Son Nhut* airport. Really sorry. It was the last day. Your dad was a good guy. He often told me about you," Marco said, moving further away from the door again.

"Really? I wasn't even a year old."

"I know. He wondered what you would grow up to be."

"Well, as you can see," Tom said, opening his hands toward some items in the store, "I've turned out fine."

"Yeah. He had lots of plans for you," Marco said. He took a deep breath and then shook his head.

"I see," is all Tom could muster.

"Listen, what I'm trying to tell you, is that it crossed my mind before, that you might be related. I drove by here a few times and saw the name on the store window."

"Why didn't you tell me all this when you first came in," Tom asked, crossing his arms.

"Don't really know. I guess I wasn't sure."

"What made you sure this time?"

"Something you and your manner is my guess. Anyway, you should know that on his last day he gave me a baby picture of you. I never got to visit your family and lost track. A shame that is," Marco said shaking his head a little.

"Why do you say that?"

"I sort of told him I would, but it was a confusing time. Anyway, Let me know when you figure out how to give me a refund," Marco said, suddenly changing course of the conversation.

Tom hesitated for a few seconds and shrugged.

"Sorry, but don't count on it."

Marco walked to the door and opened it.

"Hey, I'm just saying, you should think about it. I'll wait a few days while you make that bundle, okay? Call me when you have the money."

Marco dropped his own card next to the card holder and left, letting the door close by itself behind him.

Tom stood still for a minute, watching Marco through the window as he crossed the street. He didn't know what to think. Mercifully, his phone rang and Tom grabbed it from his desk. The call was an 800 number.

"Yeah?" Tom barked.

A woman with a pleasant voice relayed a recorded message.

"This is a courtesy call from Citibank Credit. We did not receive payment on our statement of . . ."

Tom disconnected the call. He walked around his desk and sat down, closing his eyes and running his hands through his hair, briefly resting them on his neck. He turned his gaze to the statue in the window. He picked up his phone and made a call. The moment the person on the other line picked up, Tom started talking.

"Hi, Tom here, at Arden Arts. Are you still interested in that Babylonian statue?" he asked.

The customer on the other end sounded enthusiastic.

"Of course. I love it. How much was it again?"

"Twenty five thousand."

"Okay, I'll get the money together and stop by soon."

"Great, call me when you want to pick it up. Remember, first come first serve. There's a lot of interest in it," Tom lied.

"I'll call you in a few days. If anyone else wants it, call me back."

"Right. Bye," Tom said. He moved the limp salad back in front of him and continued eating his lunch. He checked his watch. He didn't have much time to get over to Sotheby's.

CHAPTER 14

Monday Afternoon

O N HIS SECOND trip to the city that day, Tom completely rationalized his future wealth and success. The painting was a real Rembrandt judging from the reaction of Dr. Amado and his colleagues. The fact that they wanted to call in an expert was just to cover their asses, he figured. It was clear to him that it would be confirmed and then he had only one objective: sell the painting for as much money as possible. That would, for sure, be one of the largest windfalls in history, he thought. Thinking of ways to spend the money had already dominated his thoughts during most of the night. Driving on New York Ave, he paid a little more attention to traffic as he slowly came out of his temporary euphoric state. The meeting coming up was serious business and he would have to keep focused on the arrangement for the sale. There was no room to deviate from his agenda. With a big bank loan due and other bills that needed to be settled, he had very little time left to make it all happen.

He parked his car on East 72nd Street and walked around the corner to the entrance of Sotheby's. The impressive glass front always held him captive, wondering how such a fragile looking building could house such incredibly valuable pieces of art, even if it was only temporary. More than a billion dollars in art were sold here yearly and although he had never been to an auction, his friend Kevin told him all about them. A sale could be either suspenseful, fetching enormous prices and huge commissions, or duds that made them wonder why they ever took on the sale. Tom was sure that the sale of his painting would not be a dud sale and that bidders would raise one another again and again for the Rembrandt. He pushed open the door, went inside and announced himself at the reception desk.

He looked at his watch; ten minutes early. He sat down and looked outside through the glass walls. Isabelle would join him any minute. It was a short walk from the Met. He liked her to be with him in all these dealings. Unlike this morning, when she had to deal with her colleagues, this time it was her and him versus the Sotheby people. Hopefully Isabelle had done more research on the disappearance in the 1750's, because that would be helpful, and, the sooner the painting could come over from the Met, the better he figured.

Kevin walked in through a side door.

"Hey buddy. How's it going?" he asked grabbing Tom's hand and at the same time hugging him with his left arm.

"Excited," Tom said with a smile.

"I bet you are. Ready to meet the master?" he said pointing at the side door.

"Actually, Izzy's joining us," Tom said, "she's been here before and she knows your people better than I do."

"Oh, okay. No problem. She's still at the Met then?"

"Yes. Loves her job and this painting is of interest to her also."

"Maybe she'll know a little more about their findings over there."

"It's possible. They have to get an expert in though."

"That's normal," Kevin said as he turned to stand next to Tom who was still looking outside.

"Here she is," Tom said, walking to the door.

Isabelle walked in and they kissed briefly.

"Kevin, you remember Izzy, right?" Tom asked.

"Sure. Nice to see you again Isabelle," he said shaking her hand. He gestured toward the side door and they disappeared from the reception area.

Kevin took them to an elevator and into a small and impeccably decorated conference room on the ninth floor. The wood paneled walls looked as if they were freshly varnished and the sconces looked like 19th century and stood out with their golden gleam. Three of the walls had paintings on them. A Picasso was the largest and had very little paint on the canvas. A Cecilia Beaux was hanging on the opposite wall and was a portrait of a dancer. On the long wall between them there hung a frameless Warhol with more vegetables painted on it than Tom had ever cooked in his whole life. A Remington bronze that looked like *The Rattlesnake* was sitting in the middle of a rococo style massive wooden table. The six chairs matched the table and had red velour seat and back covers. Tom vaguely smelled lingering cigar smoke.

"Nice room," he said to Kevin.

"Thank you. This is where most people come to when they visit our offices," he smiled and continued. "Make yourselves comfortable. I'll go and get my boss."

Kevin left and Tom looked at Isabelle.

"Do you see all this stuff? I don't know why they haven't sold it?"

"There are always a few pieces worth keeping," she answered.

Tom chuckled, "I wonder if they're real. What do you think?"

Isabelle took a closer look and said, "Looks like it."

Tom leaned into the table and started tapping his fingers.

"I like that some things are worth keeping, and that not everything's for sale," she said after a few moments.

"Maybe," Tom said absentmindedly.

Isabelle knew that he was thinking about something else because usually he would go into a sales pitch about buying and selling. His answer was short and he was still tapping his fingers. She distracted him easily though.

"Hey, I found out where the elderly lady lives," she offered.

"Which one?" he asked.

"The one whose painting you bought."

"Oh, right, of course."

"Anyway, I called her during lunch time and she told me that the painting of the old man was indeed brought back from Germany by her late husband, after WWII."

"That explains the year 1945 on the back of the frame. Anyway, during all this time, they never checked out anything about the painting, so it's kind of too bad for them."

Isabelle did not get a chance to answer as the door opened and Jonathan Metzer walked in without knocking. Kevin followed him. Wearing a classical pin-striped navy blue suit with a silk red handkerchief poking out of the breast pocket and matching tie, he walked up to

Isabelle first as she and Tom stood up. With a wide big smile he greeted her.

"Hi, Isabelle, good to see you again. It's been a while," he said.

"Good to see you too, Jonathan. You know how it is; we don't sell that much at the Met or buy much either. We count on donations and loans. Anyway, this is Tom Arden, my boyfriend," she answered turning to Tom.

"Good to meet you, Tom," he said.

"Likewise, I have been looking forward to this meeting."

"Please, sit down," Jonathan suggested.

Once they were seated, he continued.

"So, Tom, I couldn't believe what Kevin told me this morning, it sounded incredible, but then I talked with Dr. Amado and there's a good chance you have a genuine Rembrandt."

"Yes, I'm pretty sure I do."

"Right. I also understand from Kevin that you want to offer it for sale at an auction."

"That's right. When is your next auction?"

"Well, we have one this week, but that won't work for you. You know, we have about a hundred auctions a year, but they are well planned in advance and the pieces sold have been vetted, so to speak. Also, besides announcing auctions on our web site, we bring out a catalog and it takes time to put a piece like a Rembrandt in it."

"I see. Can't you do a special auction, like within a week? Once the Dutch expert has given his blessing, we'd be all set."

Jonathan smiled and gently scratched his brown curly hair, indicating that this was going to be difficult to arrange.

"Tom, you should know that this is highly unusual, especially since we need time to get the big buyers here. Why the hurry, if I may ask?"

"It's just a matter of timing, really. I could use some funds right now."

"I see. I don't know how . . ." he said.

"Couldn't you do something like a private auction for a few people?" Tom interrupted.

"Even that takes time, unfortunately."

"I'm sure museums will really want this, so what if you picked a few and invited them?"

"Well, I'll definitely see what I can do. We really don't want to exclude other potential buyers."

"Maybe, this would be a favor to American museums. That way it will stay here and not be bought by a Chinese or Russian nouveaux-rich collector."

"I see where you're going."

"How about setting a special auction for this Friday afternoon?"

"I can discuss it internally and perhaps set a date and time, but we cannot confirm anything until the authentication process has run its course. Also, this Friday we have an *Impressionist & Modern Art* day sale and that night we feature an evening sale."

"Why don't we go on the safe assumption that it's a Rembrandt? Can we set next week then?" Tom asked.

"As I said, we will discuss it and try to get something planned, maybe for the end of next week. Please understand that we can't set a date until I have confirmed it to you, and that is also going to depend on what I hear from Dr. Amado and our own European Art curators."

"All right, then. I'll wait to hear from you. If everything works out, how does this all work? Do I bring the painting over here, and who sets a minimum price? What price would you expect to get?"

"No need to bring it here Tom. We will make the necessary security arrangement for transport with the Met. We will start the bid at five million, that is, if it's a real Rembrandt and not an original painting by a contemporary of his or one of his students. It may fetch fifteen million, perhaps even fifty million. That's why it's important to have the right bidders here. I'm not sure our own museums can afford more than thirty."

"Wow, that sounds great," Tom smiled, rubbing his hands together under the table and looking at Isabelle.

"Are you familiar with our fee schedule, Tom?" Jonathan asked, bringing Tom back to reality for a minute. It was Isabelle who answered.

"I've explained that to Tom."

"Yes, I'm okay with it. Thanks. Let's do this," Tom said and stood up.

Everyone else got up and they said goodbye. Kevin took them back to the front lobby where they parted.

"Thanks again for arranging this so quickly," Tom said to Kevin.

"No problem. Mr. Metzer will be in touch soon, I'm sure. If you need anything, you can always call me. You've got my cell," Kevin said shaking hands with both Tom and Isabelle.

They left the building and stopped on the sidewalk.

"Can you believe this? Up to fifty million!" Tom said excitedly.

"Yes I can. It'll be worth that much once it's verified and gotten the stamp of approval from the head of the Dutch Rembrandt Research Project."

"I know, I know. I'm just so excited."

"I know you are. It's going to be a while before you hear anything, so you'll need to be patient, Tom," she said gently resting her hand on his arm.

"All right," he said as he embraced her. "See you tonight around six thirty?"

"See you then," Isabelle said as she crossed the street and Tom walked back to East 72nd Street.

On the way to his car, he pulled out his phone and called his landlord who, as usual did not answer. Tom left a message.

"Luke, listen. I need another two weeks to pay up. I'll make it worthwhile to you. Call me."

CHAPTER 15

Wednesday Evening
Düsseldorf

THE CURTAINS WERE drawn and the old family room was poorly lit. A desk lamp and a light hanging from the center of the ceiling were just enough to distinguish the three people in the room. The older man was sitting in a stuffed chair, holding a cigar in his left hand. His white hair was parted on one side and mostly combed back. He wore a red bath robe with the belt undone over dark blue pajamas. He was barefoot in his leather slippers. A large Moroccan rug with intricate patterns ran from his feet to the middle of the room where a simple coffee table was covered with books and two polished yellow copper Howitzer shells. The casings reflected everything in the room as long stretched out dark lines. On the wall behind his chair, a carved, wooden version of the family crest took a prominent place. It was the typical form with a red horizontal stripe, a yellow lion above the line and a small shield with several colored lines below it. The top of the crest was adorned with small branches and leaves on which an eagle rested with one leg on a blue globe that was pierced with a white swastika.

Sitting with her back straight against the pillows, the woman on the divan was barefooted and wore a long satin bath robe. She was listening to the younger man as he leaned against the desk. He was wearing a dark suit and white shirt. His jacket was unbuttoned, and both his hands were in his pockets. His slick black hair was quite long, combed back which made him look like an artist. He finished his sentence as he looked from his father to his sister.

". . . And that's how I found out."

The old man sat up in the chair while the ashes from his cigar fell unnoticed onto the rug.

"Hans, we're so lucky you were watching that American channel when the story leaked. For years I've been looking for news about a Rembrandt. From what you just told us, I'm sure it's our painting. We cannot let it be sold," he said raising his finger in the air. "Never!"

The son agreed. "You're right father. We must and will get it back. After more than sixty five years it is time for the Rembrandt to come home."

"And you're sure that we just can't claim ownership?" his sister asked.

"Let me tell you," the old man said. "Nobody owns that painting! My father told me that the Jews had it for more than 150 years, and he never found out how exactly they got it from the House of Orange."

He took a puff on his cigar, contemplating his words while he blew the smoke out straight in front of him. He continued, "Not that it matters, it's ours now."

"But when did Uncle Helmut get the painting?" the daughter asked.

The son replied before his father could answer.

"You never heard the story? It was given to him as a reward for his services in the Great War. Isn't that right father?"

"That's what he told us, but Aunt Bertha had a different story. She claimed it was taken from a well-known Jewish family. They never claimed it before the last war. Of course, later they were transported, so there was nobody left to claim it. Aunt Bertha always said that because they never claimed it, it meant that they were not the rightful owners either," the old man said as he reclined back in his chair.

"How do you know they had it for over 150 years?" his daughter asked.

"Your uncle found a piece of paper stuck in the back of the frame with a list of rabbis dating back to 1754. Then he discovered Rembrandt's name on it when he had the painting reframed. He read that Rembrandt had painted something like it, about a hundred years before the Jews got their hands on it."

"So, if all that is true, who does have a claim on it?" the son asked.

"It belongs to whoever has it, and we have taken care of it. We kept it private. It may be worth a lot of money, but I'm not interested in selling it."

"But what about the House of Orange?" the daughter asked. "Surely, they'll find out about the painting suddenly turning up."

"The painting was inherited by the Palatine-Neuburg line of the family. When Karl III Philip died, the painting was officially lost. He was the last in the Neuburg line of the Wittelsbach family. Everyone really thought it was gone forever, but we have known better for a long time. Anyway, the House of Orange cannot claim it since that line of the family died out. Like I said, I consider the painting ours and that's it."

"That actually had been my understanding all along, father," he said.

"You know, I was only eleven years old when that American showed up at our house. If the gun hadn't jammed, I would have shot him and we would still have the Rembrandt."

"Don't beat yourself up, father. We are in this situation now and obviously, we can't let the man who has it now, sell our painting," the daughter stated.

"I've already taken action to stop that from happening," the son said while standing up and lighting a cigarette. "I contacted Fritz Schroller."

The old man sat up straight again, staring at his son.

"*The* Fritz Schroller? Where did you find him?"

"One of my contacts knew that he was hiding out in Croatia. I've talked to him already. I'm calling him now to confirm," he answered dialing a number.

The woman stood up and walked to a cabinet, getting three glasses and a bottle of Gewürztraminer.

"He will just steal it back, right?"

"Of course," her brother smiled, listening on his phone as Schroller answered his call. He turned to the side and spoke into the phone. "Yes, Fritz. You know what to do, but do it quickly and quietly."

He listened to Fritz's response.

"You'll have the money tomorrow," he said and hung up.

"So, that's settled then."

"Thank you, son," the old man said, standing up.

The son saluted his father with outstretched arm.

"Anything for the family," the son said and emptied his glass in one gulp.

CHAPTER 16

Monday Late Morning

TOM HAD FINALLY been able to arrange a meeting with Dr. Amado after a long, nervous week. He wasn't told anything on the phone, so it was with some trepidation that he entered Dr. Amado's office. Luckily, Isabelle was already there and she smiled at Tom when he shook hands with the curator.

"Please, Tom, sit down. I know you're dying to hear how things are going."

"No kidding. I've been biting my nails for a week."

"Well, we're almost there. After all our research, we're pretty close to declaring it a Rembrandt."

"That's great news," Tom almost shouted, sitting up straight in his chair.

"Everything we looked at points to the fact that the painting was produced in Rembrandt's atelier. We've got the paint matched a hundred percent and it confirms not only the date, the sixteen hundreds, but all materials, except for the stretcher frame, is from his shop. That's pretty close for us."

"What do you mean by pretty close?"

"Well, there are some things we know about Rembrandt. As was the custom in his days, anything that was painted in his atelier was his. So, if a student painted something, it was Rembrandt's property. Where it gets confusing is that often Rembrandt would add his name to it. That is obviously disturbing since that might one lead to conclude that it is a true Rembrandt. Now, to be sure, Rembrandt did not necessarily encourage his students to paint in his style, but rather coached them in the development of their own style, be it using some of his techniques.

The reason I'm saying this is that his student's paintings were different, and your painting is not."

"So, that's good news, right?"

"Yes, and there's more. We believe it's one of the seven paintings that Rembrandt supplied to the House of Orange."

"Yes, we know. You read my notes on the Stadhouder?"

"We did, and Isabelle was helpful by printing out a lot of information, saving us a lot of time. Still, we had to make sure. Here are all the things we have done so far: carbon dating, pigment analysis, thermo luminescence, as well as UV, X-ray and IT photography. There's also the fact that the painting is very similar to the etching you found. It's just larger and in mirror image. We call that a study on which the actual painting is based."

"Then we're ready to have it transported to Sotheby's?"

Dr. Amado took a deep breath and looked at both Isabelle and Tom.

"Not just yet. Remember I told you that we needed that Dutch expert to take a look at it. The earliest he can get here is tomorrow afternoon. He will spend at least a day and a half with the painting. We expect him to confirm our findings. It's just good stewardship to have the stamp of approval from the Dutch Rembrandt Research Project."

"Yes, I remember that part. Interestingly however, last week I read that the people in that group are most interested in de-authenticating "authentic" Rembrandts."

"Don't worry, Tom," Dr. Amado laughed. "I believe that in this case, they want to confirm the authenticity of the painting. This is a work of art that was lost for over 250 years. Obviously it was damaged by a fire in the past. This reduces the probability of it being a forgery."

"Okay, so he could be ready by Wednesday?"

"Normally speaking, yes, and I hate to do this to you. Tom, but . . ."

"Not another hurdle, I hope," Tom interrupted.

"It's a small one. In this day and age we would be fools not to use the latest technology to help us confirm what we already think. I'm not sure whether you know this, Tom, but at one point we thought that over seven hundred Rembrandts had survived. Using the experience of experts and new scientific methods we now know with a high degree of certainty that about half of those paintings are by Rembrandt. The rest are by students, contemporaries, etc. So, we still have one process to go through."

"How long will that take?" Tom asked almost in desperation, having lost that edge of excitement in his voice.

"It can be done by Thursday. I know you want it for the auction on Friday, and it should not be a problem to get it to Sotheby's in time."

"So who is doing that last test then?"

"It's actually a mathematical process involving pattern recognition. This work will be done by Dr. Stockton of NYU. Here is his card in case you have any questions."

Tom took the card and stared at it briefly. He tapped a pencil on the table. Isabelle had been quiet and knew that Tom was bothered by this whole authentication process because it took so much time. She decided to introduce the worst case scenario now, so that Dr. Amado could hopefully refute it.

"What happens if it isn't a Rembrandt after all?" she asked.

"While we're pretty sure it's not by one of his students and it's not a forgery, it would be an enormous discovery if we found out there was another master of that period who had that style of painting. Just about impossible," Dr. Amado laughed.

"Well, that about settles it," she said, looking at Tom who seemed less stressed.

"I'll give your telephone number to Dr. Stockton if that's okay with you," Dr. Amado said, turning to Tom.

"No problem," he said.

It was suddenly quiet as neither Isabelle nor Dr. Amado had anything to add to that. It was only for a few seconds and then the silence was broken as Tom snapped his pencil in two. Isabelle gently put her hand on Tom's arm.

"It'll be okay Tom, I've heard that Dr. Stockton is very efficient and you really need to get all these stamps of approval."

"All right then," Tom said standing up. "Dr. Amado, thank you for your time. Please call me as soon as the expert and Dr. Stockton have confirmed once and for all that I have a Rembrandt."

Dr. Amado got up and shook Tom's hand, showing him to the door.

"Rest assured, Tom, I will call you immediately."

Outside the building, Tom put his arm around Isabelle's waist and pulled her closer as they walked toward his car.

"They're making this difficult for me," he said. "Why wasn't he up front with us last week? He knew what's involved in an authentication process. The longer it takes, the more there is a chance that one of these experts had some doubt."

"Tom, cut it out!" Isabelle said suddenly stopping. "You're being ridiculous. The only thing that's delaying the process is the fact that the expert from Holland couldn't jump on a plane last week. That is understandable."

"Yes, but I have a feeling we won't make it by Friday," Tom sulked.

"Hey, the Met is interested in the painting too, you know. They might just buy it at the auction. Let's get some lunch."

They decided to go to a place near Wall Street. Tom had insisted on driving. It gave him a sense of control. During the drive, he was mulling everything over from the morning, and didn't speak to Isabelle. Nearing Church Street, he ran his second red light.

"Watch out Tom!" Isabelle yelled. "We're not in a hurry for lunch."

"I'm sorry. I just can't stop worrying. Money is real tight now and I need any sale I can as soon as possible."

"I understand, but try to be patient."

As he slowed down near an open parking spot, Tom looked in his rearview mirror. If he had done that earlier instead of being pre-occupied and neglecting traffic, he might have noticed the black Mercedes that had followed him all the way from the museum.

As they walked toward the restaurant, Tom finally opened up.

"You know, Izzy, I really need this auction to happen soon. Right now I don't have enough money to pay the damn bank on Monday."

"How about that Babylonian statue? You're close to selling that, right?" she asked.

"I have no paperwork, remember? There's just a tag and the guy who got hold of it during the looting told me the name of the Baghdad Museum is on it in Arabic."

"Christ, Tom! You never told me it was stolen. You've got to return it. You get caught with that and you're done! You can't sell that to anybody."

"Easy for you to say! Let someone else worry about it. I paid five big ones for it. The buyer's already agreed with the amount. It just won't be enough to settle my financial problems. Don't worry, the statue is a good deal. Let's go inside.'

The Mercedes parked on the other side of the road. The driver stayed inside.

CHAPTER 17

Monday Late Afternoon

AFTER DROPPING ISABELLE off at the Met, Tom returned to the store. He wanted to make sure he was there in case the client who wanted the small painting in the window came in. He had already waited for him a few times last week, and again, the client hadn't shown up yet. While he waited, he had researched the mathematical techniques used in the authentication of paintings and was overwhelmed with the information he found. Every time he finished a topic, he would stop and look at the picture of his Rembrandt he had taken with his iPhone. One technique involved high resolution digital images and complex mathematical formulas. It evolved from pattern recognition in analyzing features in a person's photograph, reducing the observations to mathematical equations. Reading about how artists tended to favor certain proportions and angles in people's faces and bodies, Tom began to understand that indeed, this differed from one painter to another. When he was taking art classes in college, they had not covered this at all. He found it interesting that using these techniques, one could distinguish easily between two artists who painted similarly by measuring the ratio of the distance between the eyes and the distance from the eyebrow line to the bottom of the chin. He read that artists also favor certain angles in landscape compositions. Statistical analysis based on ratios, angles and tonal variations provided a solid insight into how a painter worked. It reduced a painting to a set of probabilities and numbers. What could go wrong? Tom thought.

It was Luke's call that tore him away from his reading on the scientific analysis to which his painting was about to be subjected.

"Arden Arts," he answered.

"Tom, Luke here. Got your message."

"Good. You're okay with it then?"

"What did you mean by making it worthwhile?"

"I'm coming into some money and as soon . . ."

"Yeah, yeah. Heard that one too many times. As I said . . ."

"No really! This is big money. I'll pay you not only the rent I owe and some interest, but the rest of the year in advance."

"You're fucking killing me, Tom."

"I swear it, man. You'll see. Give me until a week from today."

"I don't know why I should, but okay. This is your last chance. I'm moving you out on Tuesday if you don't pay up."

"You won't need to," Tom said, ending the call.

He checked his watch and figured he had time for one more call and then he would head to his apartment. There was no answer, but he left a message anyway.

"Hi, this is Tom at Arden Arts. I still have that small painting you were interested in. Maybe you can stop by tomorrow during your lunch break. I'll be in. I think I can get a better price for you."

He locked the store and drove home.

Tom parked his car near his apartment since all the spaces in front were taken. He locked the door and turned away toward his building. A large man blocked his way. He had blond hair, a tanned square face with a small scar on his left cheek. He wore jeans and a tight black T-shirt under a black leather jacket.

"Excuse me," Tom said.

The man stepped aside, but as Tom hurried by him, the man spoke to him.

"Not so fast," he yelled as he threw away a partly smoked small cigar.

Tom briefly looked over his shoulder but walked on. The man yelled a little louder. Tom distinctly heard a German accent.

"You don't know me, but I have a hundred thousand dollars for you."

Tom stopped and turned around.

"Yeah right, buddy. Leave me alone," he said starting to walk away.

The man would not leave him alone.

"I know about that Rembrandt."

This time Tom stopped on a dime and slowly turned around. "What do you know about it?"

"Aha! So you do have the painting."

"Fuck off, buddy!"

"I guess you don't know that there's someone who owns that painting, right?"

"Nobody but me owns it."

"My contact in Germany doesn't think so. It was stolen from him. He can make your life miserable," the man said, walking closer to Tom.

Tom was feeling both uncomfortable and annoyed. How did this stranger know about the painting and what did he mean by his threat?"

"If something's stolen, go to the police."

"We would rather handle this quietly so you won't be embarrassed."

"I don't embarrass easily, fellow. What's your name?"

"Not important. I'm only the messenger and we want to handle this discreetly."

"Really? That's why you stop me here in the middle of the sidewalk to discuss something discreetly? Give me a fucking break."

"No need to get upset, Mr. Arden. It's Tom, right?"

"Tell your contact I'm not interested in any discreet deal."

"You can have a hundred thousand in cash tomorrow if you give it to me."

"You're an idiot. It's worth a lot more."

"I wouldn't be so sure. You may be surprised."

"Oh yeah? I can get more at an auction this Friday. Then what are you going to do? Chase whoever has the painting then? Good luck, jerk!"

"No one will buy a basically worthless painting. At least I am offering a hundred thousand. You have until tomorrow evening, same time."

"Hey, you show up wherever you want, whenever you want, but you won't find me with the painting unless you go the auction on Friday. I don't have it anyway. It's in good hands at the Metropolitan."

Schroller remained calm and lit up another small cigar.

"Be here tomorrow. You'll regret it in many ways if you don't."

Tom laughed at him. Was this guy trying to extort him? And if there was someone who supposedly owned the painting, why hadn't he come forward before? He laughed at the man.

"Go on, get out of here. You're fucking crazy," he said and walked up to the building.

Schroller did not bother to answer and got into his Mercedes. Tom noticed the license plate as the car took off. He shrugged his shoulders as he put his key in the door lock.

Inside the apartment, Tom read through the statement and the letter he had received from the bank. His phone rang.

"This is Tom," he said absentmindedly staring at the paperwork

"Marco here. Wanted to know if we were still on track."

"Well, I'm doing my job, that's all."

"Good. Now, just don't go ripping off the next guy to pay me."

"I didn't tell you I ripped off anyone or that I was going to pay you."

Marco changed the subject looking for Tom's vulnerable spots.

"Did you take care of that registration today?"

"Listen, stay out of my business, all right?" Tom said without waiting for an answer and pushing *End* on his phone.

The call added to his frustration. He sat down, running his fingers through his hair. He shook his head as if he was trying to get rid of the negative thoughts in his head. He dialed Isabelle's number.

"Hey, Izzy. You won't believe what happened tonight."

"What happened?"

"I got home and before I got to the apartment building, this guy walks up to me and . . ." Tom said walking to a comfortable sofa.

He told Isabelle about how he turned down a hundred thousand dollars.

CHAPTER 18

Tuesday Morning

TOM HAD GOTTEN to the office early that day. He went through Monday's mail and saw that the bank had sent to the office the same letter he had received at home. He read the letter again. In it, the bank representative came right to the point. Tom was behind on his loan, and the bank requested that the entire remaining amount of ninety five thousand dollars be paid in full no later than the close of business, next Monday. The letter mentioned the collateral which consisted mostly of the inventory of the store. It's a lot worth more than that, he figured, but if the bank were to act on the letter, he basically would have nothing left. The auction on Friday really had to save him. If it was postponed because of the authentication process, he'd have to have a plan B and the only way plan B would work was if he started on it right away. He put the letter in his drawer and took out the stack of index cards that represented his inventory. He looked at each card carefully and put those not representing imminent deals aside on his desk. With five cards left in his hand, he picked each matching item on the cards from the display and put them on his desk. He wiped off the vase and put it in the middle. He put the statue and the small painting to the left, and to the right he placed a small bronze and a Greek Icon. He added up the potential sum from the cards: one hundred and twenty five thousand dollars. That would cover his immediate debt. It was especially necessary to sell the vase and the Babylonian statue.

Tom picked up his phone, ready to call the people who had shown interest in the items, but a client walked in so he put the phone back down

"Hi, good morning. I was hoping you would be open."

"Yes, yes. Of course. Come right in," Tom said.

"I'm here for the Ming vase," the man said.

"Perfect. I've just gotten it ready for you."

"I'd like to look at it one more time, if you don't mind," the man said, reaching with both hands for the vase.

"Go ahead," Tom said moving the Greek Icon and the statue out of the way.

The man studied the vase and then turned it upside down. On the bottom he found a blue square with several Chinese characters painted inside. He compared it to images in a small booklet he had brought along.

Tom was curious.

"Is there something I can help you with?" he asked.

The man squinted, looked at the mark again and shook his head.

"I'm just not finding the *nian huo* in my reference book," he said.

Tom heard his disappointment but did not want this to be a deal breaker. It would be a great start of the day if he could sell this vase right now.

"You mean the mark?" he asked.

"Yes. Maybe I just missed it in this little book. Can I take a picture of it?"

"Sure, but I may have a book here you can find it in," Tom offered.

As Tom walked to the bookcase, the door opened again. Tom looked over his shoulder, hoping for another client, but only saw Marco who walked over to the display window.

Immediately, Tom was annoyed and took the client to a corner of the store, whispering, "We can talk more confidentially over here."

The man started looking through his reference book again, since Tom had not yet found his own book.

"I assure you, this is a real Ming vase," Tom continued.

"I believe you, but before I plunk down the sixty grand, I need to confirm the mark. I'll call you tomorrow," the man said, wondering about the need for secrecy.

"You really don't need to call me. Look, I have the papers here," Tom said, showing him the Chinese document, and pointed to the matching mark. "These are the official papers. This is the Ming mark that corresponds with the one on the vase. And these are the authentic papers from China."

"I see. Well, maybe it's all right then. This is a serious investment, so this is important to me," the man said, giving the papers back to Tom.

"Oh, you'll be very happy with the vase. It's in the best possible condition. It's a rare masterpiece. You will be paying by check I assume?" he asked as if the deal was done.

The man however, was still hesitant.

"Most likely. I need a little more time though. I'll come back when I'm ready to buy it."

"Okay, fine, but I can't hold it for you too long," Tom said, using his standard reply when a customer needed a little push. This time, it didn't work. The man simply said that he'd be back and walked out of the store.

Tom turned toward Marco.

"Didn't I tell you last night to stay out of my business?"

"I was in the area and wanted to see how you were doing."

"I'm fine. Listen, I need to go. I have a meeting downtown."

"Good. I hope it's a good one," he said with a faint smile, and continued. "Anyway, it sounded like that guy was a little suspicious about that vase."

Tom grabbed his jacket and with his keys in his hand, moved toward the door.

"How so?"

"He thinks it's not the real thing. Is it?"

"Of course it is. I have the paperwork."

"How about that big deal I heard you talking about last week?"

"It's still on track," Tom said, opening the door.

"Now, you're sure you can really sell it. You don't want to screw another customer."

"I'm not screwing a customer. No, the painting is legit. The Met people said so."

"What I mean is, you didn't cheat someone out of that painting, did you? Why is it such a big deal?"

"If you really want to know, it's a very old and possibly valuable painting by a famous Dutch painter. I've got the sales receipt."

"That does sound like a big deal," Marco said, stepping outside. "If you can sell that, it would take care of a lot of things, wouldn't it? And, if it's not, well, trouble is just around the corner."

"No problem. I've got everything under control," Tom said, locking the door and walking to his car without another word to Marco.

A short while later Tom arrived at the museum. Since the meeting the week before at Sotheby's, there was something Isabelle said that sat in the back of his mind. The Met, with its vast resources and wealth in paintings, was sometimes not in a position to purchase a valuable painting. They had tons of artwork that were stored but did not exhibit. If they were really interested in another masterpiece by one of the greatest painters, why not unload some of those pieces? He'd have to ask Isabelle why they didn't sell that stuff. In any case, she had also indicated that they took paintings on loan. That had piqued his interest. If they could not pay for a masterpiece, but wanted it in their museum, they could loan it from whoever will have bought the painting on Friday. He wondered how much they would pay for something like that. He needed to find out.

As Tom drove to the museum, the German followed in the Mercedes. Tom, as usual, had been too busy to notice since he was on the phone most of the time and so many things were going through this mind. Sometimes he wondered how he got from one point to another without remembering a thing about it.

At the Met, Schroller walked in shortly after Tom had entered the lobby. He noticed that someone took Tom up in an elevator and he decided to do some investigation. He knew that the painting was somewhere in this building, perhaps not as well guarded as the artwork in an exhibition. He figured they were still studying it. If only he knew where. Not wanting to attract too much attention he walked over to a display on the wall with the floor plan. After studying it for a few minutes, he walked up the staircase to the second floor toward the European Art section, just missing another visitor to the museum who was greeted and taken into the same elevator Tom had disappeared with. The Dutch expert had arrived.

Schroller was slowly strolling through the permanent exhibition and stopped at one of the Rembrandt paintings. He had never seen one before and did not grasp why his contact thought they were so great. Looking closer at *Aristotle with a Bust of Homer* he tried to figure out what the big deal was. He looked around and saw several people slowly walking from one painting to the next. He spotted a guard, standing near a door, hands clasped behind his back. He walked over.

"Are there any bathrooms on this floor?" he asked.

The guard pointed to a hallway across from the Musical Instruments section. Stepping into the hallway, Schroller noticed that the guard was called away and he quickly opened a door that lead into a larger hallway.

There was a room on his left and he casually checked to see whether the door was locked. It wasn't. He continued down the hallway and as he turned a corner, he noticed two men at the very end shaking hands. He was only thirty feet away and took a step back behind the corner and listened. Dr. Amado was welcoming his guest.

"Thanks for coming Mr. van Weteren. I hope your trip will have been worthwhile."

"I hope so too. The Rembrandt Research Project is eager to see the painting," van Weteren said.

"Please follow me. I want you to meet someone," Dr. Amado said, heading toward Schroller.

Schroller took a few more steps back and walked unseen into the room he just checked. He closed the door quickly and held his breath. Dr. Amado and van Weteren had moved into the adjoining room. The two rooms were separated by a temporary wall that folded back if there was a need to make it a larger room. Schroller now breathed a sigh of relief and walked closer to the dividing wall so he could better hear the conversation in the other half of the room.

"Mr. Van Weteren, this is Dr. Stockton of NYU," Dr. Amado said.

Van Weteren and Stockton shook hands and politely said hello. Dr. Amado smiled. He knew that these two men approached authentication in a totally different way, but they respected each other.

"Dr. Stockton is scanning the painting tomorrow and will do the mathematical analysis himself," Dr. Amado said.

"Yes, we'll do the scan here and take the files to my office at NYU and run the analysis there. I should be finished by Thursday morning. I'll work day and night if I have to."

"That is good," van Weteren said, nodding his head, and then turned to Dr. Amado. "I hope we reach the same conclusion about the Rembrandt?"

"That would be perfect. Shall I take you to the painting in the restoration room?"

"I can't wait," van Weteren said as he and Dr. Stockton followed Dr. Amado out of the room.

In the adjoining room, Schroller waited a few seconds by the door. When he heard the other door close, he carefully peeked out and saw the three men go around the corner. He quickly left the room and followed. Looking carefully around the corner he saw Dr. Amado use a digital card to get access to a door and the men disappeared behind it. Schroller dashed for the door, but it closed just before he got there and he heard the lock engage. Upset at having missed his chance to get to the painting, he walked back to the Instrument section. He went downstairs and waited in the lobby for Tom.

The director's door opened slowly as Tom stopped and turned to the man in charge of the Metropolitan Museum. They shook hands and the director made one more point.

"Thanks for the suggestion, Mr. Arden."

"No problem," Tom said smiling. "I'll see you on Friday then, one way or the other."

"At the auction."

"Correct. I assume the date won't change. I'll contact Metzer about all this."

"And I'll inform Dr. Amado."

"Understood. Have a good day," Tom said closing the door and headed for the elevator. There was definitely a spring in his step. Once downstairs in the lobby, he smiled at everyone, flung his jacket over his shoulder and walked out, not noticing Schroller who followed him.

CHAPTER 19

Tuesday Evening

THE RESTAURANT WAS known as *the* Italian bistro to go to in Queens. The owner was born in Italy. After several jobs aboard cruise ships, he ended up in New York and started a successful restaurant. He was a hands-on type of guy in the kitchen as well as in the dining room. He still spoke with a heavy Italian accent, accompanying his words with plenty of hand and arm movements to stress or refute a point. Tom had never been able to figure out whether the accent was real or not. Of course it added to the atmosphere and was quite charming. Patrons felt at home in this very authentic Italian restaurant. The whole place exuded calmness with dim lighting, candles on white linen covered tables, and soft Italian opera music in the background. Tom and Isabelle agreed that this was their favorite restaurant in the borough and came in at least twice a month. They had gotten to know the owner well and he greeted them warmly when they entered. He knew Isabelle's particular requests and always personally brought a glass of lukewarm water with lemon to the table as soon as they were seated. Tom had the regular water with ice and invariably asked to see the wine list, though he normally ordered a bottle of Valpolicella.

Tonight was no different and they enjoyed a mid-week dinner out. Their waiter had just served the appetizers and Tom toasted to the upcoming auction.

"I heard you were at the Met today," Isabelle said after his toast. "Did you meet with Dr. Amado and the Rembrandt expert?"

"No, I think they were in a meeting. I was in the area and figured I'd stop by to see whether there was any more news," Tom said, looking at the label on the bottle.

"And you didn't stop by my office?"

"I didn't have much time. I waited for a while for Dr. Amado, but left," he lied.

"I see . . . Say, what happened to that hundred thousand dollar you were supposed to meet with?" Isabelle asked. "Wasn't that this evening?"

"Forget him! Why would I even think about 100K when I've got millions coming my way? I'm sure he gave up on me. He can take his claim to whoever has the painting next."

"From what you said though, he sounded more like a guy who wouldn't take *no* for an answer."

Tom took a forkful of salad and looked up.

"I wouldn't worry about it. He tried and he failed."

"I hope you're right," Isabelle said, taking a sip of wine. "Anyway, as I was trying to say, Mr. van Weteren arrived today."

"That's the Dutch expert, right?"

"The very one. He's actually quite a famous man. You should read up on him on Wikipedia. If he says it's a Rembrandt, it really is."

"You see, that's what bothers me, Izzy. Here is a guy who's an expert in identifying whether a painting is a Rembrandt or not. He has this Rembrandt Research Project group to back him up and that's all fine. What happens however, when the scientific expert comes along and says it's not a Rembrandt? What's Dr. Amado going to say then, and how can I ever sell it at an auction? At Sotheby's they're not going to auction off something that's in doubt right?"

"You still don't trust that scientific process do you? I agree that sometimes there are different opinions, but it is not as severe as that. It's more like one expert saying that he's a hundred percent sure, while the other expert says the certainty is around ninety percent. It's almost never like a high and low percentage. Believe me, they're usually very close and when they both get to over ninety percent, it's a done deal."

"Well, let's hope so," Tom said, putting his fork down.

"I also think that Dr. Amado's initial observation is a solid indication. You said so yourself last week after he had his first look at it."

"I guess you're right. I just think that more tests increase the chance that some crummy expert come around and will pronounce it a forgery or something."

"Don't worry. It'll be all over in a few days," Isabelle said, as the waiter brought the main course.

It was close to ten when Tom unlocked the door to his apartment. Isabelle turned on a light and dropped her purse on the couch. Tom headed straight for the kitchen where he kept his cognac and whiskey. Isabelle grabbed his arm and pulled him back. She kissed him gently.

"No more drinks!" she insisted.

"Wow, the lady's on a mission," Tom said, taking off his jacket.

Isabelle smiled and led him to the bedroom. Tom wanted to close the door and turn on the light, but Isabelle started to laugh.

"C'mon now, it's just us, there's enough light from the hallway."

Tom didn't say anything and took Isabelle firmly in his arms, kissing her softly on the lips at first, but then more intensely. He moved his right hand to the top of her dress, feeling for the zipper. Not breaking their kiss, he slowly unzipped her black dress letting it slip off her shoulders and onto a puddle on the floor. He put his hand on her bra clasp, but Isabelle backed off a little.

"Take it easy. Slow down," she whispered, kissing him and unbuttoning his shirt, button by button, taking her time. She pulled his shirt out of his pants to undo the last button, opening his shirt wide. She put her hands on his chest and moved them from his chest to his abdomen and around his lower back. Tom took off his shirt while they continued kissing. Isabelle kicked off her shoes and Tom pushed his loafers off. He pressed hard against Isabelle who edged them closer to the bed. When she felt the bed she broke their kiss, sat down and with Tom still standing, she undid his belt buckle and unzipped his pants. Tom performed a little dance, getting out of his pants. They laughed when he fell onto the bed. Tom pulled Isabelle on top of him. Their kissing was more passionate now. Not hearing Isabelle protest this time, Tom unsnapped her bra. She lifted up a little to take the straps off her shoulders and flung her bra away. It landed in the doorway. Tom rolled with Isabelle so that he was on top. He gently caressed one shoulder, moved his right hand to her breast and then toward her hips. Isabelle moaned seductively as her hands slid down Tom's back.

Both were oblivious to a shadowy movement in the doorway. Schroller observed for a few seconds and then coughed lightly.

"Having fun?"

Isabelle shrieked and Tom rolled off her, sitting up immediately. Isabelle slid out of the bed, away from the door, landing on the floor. Tom jumped out of bed.

"What the fuck?"

Tom lunged toward Schroller to hit him, but Schroller moved aside quickly and pounded a fist into Tom's diaphragm. Tom fell to the ground, gulping for air. Schroller then kicked him in the side making Tom pull his legs up in pain, assuming the fetal position. Isabelle yelled his name. Tom couldn't say anything. While he held one foot on Tom's shoulder, Schroller turned his attention to Isabelle who was still hiding on the other side of the bed. She looked frantically for a phone.

"So, where are you hiding?" Schroller asked, lighting a cigarillo. "Come on out, because this guy here isn't going to stop me from coming to get you."

Isabelle sat up on her knees so that Schroller could see only her head and shoulders.

"Leave us alone? Who are you?"

"Ah, *Fraulein*, I'm sorry. My name is Schroller and I came to claim a painting. You see, this is what happens when your boyfriend here doesn't deliver. I waited with the cash for a long time tonight. So, instead of the painting, maybe I should take you with me, *ja*?" he asked, grinning.

While Schroller was paying more attention to Isabelle, Tom started to breathe regularly. Neglecting the pain in his side, he grabbed Schroller's leg and tried to pull him down.

"I told you the painting's not here!" he yelled.

Schroller kicked Tom until he had to let go of his leg.

"Get ready to go and get it with me!"

"Are you stupid? It's in the museum like I told you. It's closed. Get the fuck out of here, and leave us alone," Tom screamed.

While they talked, Isabelle had put on Tom's shirt that earlier he flung on the other side of the bed. She crawled to the end of the bed and took Tom's pants. She retrieved his phone from a pocket, started dialing, looked up and saw Schroller staring at her.

"Throw that phone over here," he yelled, pointing a gun at her.

Isabelle threw it on the bed toward Schroller. Keeping the gun pointed at her, he kicked Tom again in the ribs.

"Get up," he commanded, clearly in charge now with a gun. "Go stand with her."

Tom was getting up but remained hunched over, holding his arms across his belly and chest. He sat on his knees when he reached the other side of the bed. Isabelle put her arm around him and she was shaking.

Schroller picked up the phone and dialed his own number on Tom's phone, pointing the gun at them.

"Now you have my number and I have yours," he said throwing the phone back on the bed. He bent down and picked up Isabelle's bra.

"Get the painting by ten tomorrow morning. I'll call you with the details. No police. This time you'd better be there."

He picked up Isabelle's bra, twirled it in the air, and threw it on the bed. He dropped the cigarillo on the floor and crushed it with his heel.

"So, let me remind you: it's delivery or take-out! You deliver the painting, or I do the taking out. Don't get up. I'll let myself out."

Schroller left, slamming the bedroom door behind him. Tom got up slowly, trying to walk to the door, and stopped briefly. Taking a deep breath he grimaced and opened the door.

"Tom, no! He has a gun!" Isabelle yelled.

Tom turned around. "I want to make sure he's gone. Stay here."

When Tom entered the living room, Schroller had already closed the apartment door. Tom double locked the door and put the chain in the slot before he went back to the bedroom.

"I just wanted to make sure the door was locked."

Isabelle was sitting on the floor against a wall with her knees pulled up and her arms around them. She just nodded and Tom pulled her up, putting his arm around her, holding her tightly.

"He's gone Izzy. We're okay now. Do you want a glass of water?"

"Yes, please," she said.

Tom put his pants back on and together they walked to the kitchen. Tom filled a glass and gave it to Isabelle.

"I'm shaking Tom. This is serious. We need to call the police."

"He said no cops. I've got to figure something out to get rid of this guy."

"He's dangerous and we need to call the police," Isabelle said, holding on to Tom.

"He's gone for now," Tom said. His mind was whirling, trying to find a way to deal with all of this. If the police were to get involved, too much attention would be brought to the painting. What if Schroller could create doubt about the ownership of his Rembrandt? The auction could be postponed and, in the worst case, the painting could even be taken away from him. No police! There must be a different way, he thought.

"How did he get in here?" Isabelle asked.

"No idea. Maybe he picked the lock," Tom said.

"Can't the police arrest him for breaking and entering?"

"If they can find him, maybe. No, the police can't help us right now," he answered and immediately snapped his fingers. "But I do know someone who can," he said, walking back to the bedroom to collect his phone and his jacket.

"Who're you going to call?" Isabelle called out while she sat down at the kitchen table.

Tom returned, fishing a business card out of his jacket pocket.

"A detective. Actually, an ex-detective," he said. "I bet he'll know how to handle this guy."

Tom dialed the number.

"Now that the discovery of the painting was on the news the past few days, there may be more crazies that want at it," Isabelle said.

Tom nodded and grimaced briefly, holding his stomach. He heard Marco's greeting and left a message, asking him to call back as soon as possible, regardless of the time.

"Yes, I know," Tom said, ending the call. "Kevin put it on his blog and it just blew up."

"You're the one who sent him the picture."

"I know, I know. Too late now. I'm sure this detective will figure out how to take care of the guy when he shows up tomorrow," Tom said, walking over to the sink, filling up a glass of water for himself.

"This guy's not getting the painting!" Isabelle said firmly.

"Hell no," Tom said, sitting down at the kitchen table across from Isabelle. His phone rang.

"Marco?" he guessed.

"Yeah. What's up?"

"We had an intruder in my apartment. He was after that painting I mentioned to you."

"Wow. That's serious, have you called the police?" Marco asked.

"Not yet, it just happened. We're still in shock. Can you come over to my apartment?" Tom asked. "It's about eight blocks from the office on 7241 Murray Avenue, apartment B. We need your help."

"Give me ten minutes," Marco said and hung up.

"Let's get dressed, he's coming over," Tom said, getting up from the table.

Tom was sitting by himself in the living room when Marco knocked on the door. Tom walked over and opened it.

"Thanks for coming."

"No problem. For a minute there, I thought you were going to pay up," Marco smiled.

"Sorry about that," Tom said, feeling a little uncomfortable. "Like I said on the phone, I need to know what to do about this guy. I didn't tell you, but yesterday he offered me 100K cash for the painting. I was supposed to meet him tonight with it, but I didn't show up."

"You didn't take his offer?"

"Of course not! The 100K doesn't even come close to the real value of the painting. It's my ticket to becoming rich."

"How did he find out you have the painting?"

"It was on the news that a Rembrandt was found. My name never came up, so it beats me how he knew that I own it. He said he has been hired to get it back to the rightful owner in Germany."

"You should have told me this yesterday."

"I didn't think it was necessary," Tom said, lifting his shoulders slightly.

"I asked if it was clean, and now there's another owner?"

"The guy has it wrong, the Metropolitan and I investigated it. It's mine."

"All right, so what are you going to do?"

"I figured that as a detective, you could help me deal with this guy. Look, when I sell the painting, I'll pay you double what you think I owe you."

"I don't know what I'm getting into here, Tom. Remember, I'm a bit rusty. I've been retired a few years."

"He told me no cops, so you're the only help we have right now. I've already been beaten up by the guy and he pointed his gun at my girlfriend, Isabelle. She's in the bedroom. She'll be out soon. She's been crying."

"I understand," Marco nodded.

"So, can you help us?"

"Frankly, if I were you, I'd go to the cops. At least you can report a breaking and entering and they can put an APB out on the guy."

"Maybe. But you can help catch him."

"And how would I do that?"

"I'm supposed to meet him tomorrow to give him the painting."

"I see," Marco said slowly, as if contemplating helping Tom. He didn't mind giving advice, but to get involved in someone else's mess with a criminal of this caliber, was not a good idea.

"Does that mean you'll help us?"

"Not so fast. As I said, I have no idea of what I'm getting into."

"I'll pay you double Marco," Tom said. If this implicitly sounded like admitting he overcharged Marco, it did not register with Tom. It did, however, with Marco.

Marco sat back in the chair. He tapped his fingers on the arm rest, thinking. Then from his inside pocket of his jacket he took out a small notepad and a pen. He sighed.

"All right, I'll see what I can do. I'll have to let the police know and you need to file the B&E tonight."

"Okay. So, we have a deal?"

"Sure, I'll take your deal. But, with what's going on, you might not have a painting to sell. Anyway, I'm doing it more because I told your dad I'd look you up after the war. If I had never set foot in your shop, I'd still feel bad about that after all these years. So I'm making good on an old promise. That's all, and just this one time, understood?"

"Sure, thanks," Tom said relieved that he would not have to face Schroller all alone.

Leaning forward now, Marco started his old routine of getting the facts.

"What did the guy look like?" was his first question.

"Tall and blond, kind of a square face, in his thirties and he definitely had a German accent," Tom said.

"Right. Now, did he mention anything else besides the painting?"

"Nope, that's it."

"Was he driving a car yesterday?"

"Yeah, a black Mercedes."

"License plate by any chance?"

"Got it here," Tom said, looking at a piece of paper on the table. "LXX-9491."

"Anything peculiar you noticed about him?"

"No . . . Wait, yes, the bastard put his little cigar out on my bedroom floor. I put it in a tissue on the counter here."

"Can I have it?"

Tom handed the tissue to Marco who held the stub under his nose.

"A cigarillo. A Dutch Masters I think. My neighbor smokes these."

"Is that important?"

"Maybe."

"So, he wants to meet you tomorrow?"

"Yeah, by ten."

"Where?"

"He's going to call me with the place for the exchange."

"Right. We'll have the cops stake out that place once you know where it is."

"He said no cops," Tom said, turning toward the bedroom. He heard a door being closed.

Isabelle came through the small hallway and joined them. Marco got up.

"You must be Isabelle," Marco said, introducing himself. "I'm Marco Vincente," he said, shaking hands with her.

"Glad to meet you. Now, what was that about the police?"

"All kidnappers say no to police involvement."

"I thought about calling the cops too, but while I took a shower I figured that would just escalate things and I don't want Tom caught in the middle of some shootout."

"I know what you're saying, but the police know what they're doing. I would go ahead and report the breaking and entering."

"We will, but I don't want the painting to become evidence in their investigation," Tom said.

"I don't think that'll be an issue. There are two ways they can catch the guy. When they see him near the drop zone, they can get him and arrest him on the B&E; or once the exchange has been made, they can catch him with the painting. In that case it would be evidence, but I'm sure they would return it to you within 48 hours."

Tom got up and rubbed his chin.

"Well, there's a problem. Experts at the Metropolitan Museum are busy working with the painting because it needs authentication. If I take it away to use in the exchange, it'll halt that process and I may not make the auction by Friday."

"Tom's right," Isabelle added. "They could miss it for a few hours perhaps, but not longer."

Tom sat down again.

"What happens if the guy takes off with the painting? What if the first option doesn't pan out and they fail to get him? This guy is smart."

"That's a small risk," Marco said.

"What would you do if we don't involve the police in the exchange at all?" Isabelle asked.

"Well, both options are still there, except that I would need to get the guy before the exchange. Not being a detective anymore, there is no way that I can arrest him. I can maybe detain him for a short while."

"Yes, but once you have him, the police can make the arrest, right?" Tom tried to help the thought process along.

"We might as well involve them from the start then," Marco said.

"All right, why can't you arrange that they stay away from the exchange and wait for your call once you have the guy?" Tom asked.

"It's still a dangerous proposition. The man is armed and this could go all wrong," Marco said.

"I think the police needs to be your backup. The German can't see any police or he would run and then you may not get him," Isabelle said.

"Okay, you call the cops about the B&E now. I'm going to the precinct and make the arrangement. I'll see you in the morning at your store. Make sure you have the painting by nine," Marco said.

CHAPTER 20

Wednesday Morning

TOM WALKED TO the store carrying a package under his arm. On the door he found a taped, handwritten message. It was from Luke. Tom called him an asshole, crumpled up the paper and once inside, threw it in his waste paper basket. He put the package on a chair and made sure his phone was charged. He had not slept well. When he did sleep, he dreamt that Marco, being under no obligation whatsoever to help him, did not show up at all. Isabelle also had a rough night and although she didn't complain of nightmares, she was restless all night long. The one time he had gotten up, she asked him to check whether the door was double locked. She had gotten up around six and had left for her apartment. After that he hadn't been able to fall asleep again. He worried about whether Marco would follow through with the plan. He had been tempted to call him but stopped short, realizing it had just been a dream.

At the store, Tom left the *Closed* sign on the door. He would be leaving soon and it was too early for anyone besides Marco to be coming by. He sat down at his desk and checked his top inventory index cards again. Granted, if he could sell the top five items and if he took the 100K from Schroller, the total amount would tide him over well, paying the bank, the landlord and various other creditors. Of course, giving Schroller a painting for a mere 100K was crazy. Even he had to know that it wasn't a forgery, otherwise why would anyone pay that kind of money for some paint on a canvas that was crafted by someone else. No, the painting was real and that's what the experts were going to conclude. Nevertheless, Schroller had to be dealt with and he really hoped that Marco was the guy to pull it off. Tom had thought about his deal with Marco earlier that morning and realized that by offering it, he may have alluded to the fact that he had charged him too much for that document. Not that he was going to admit that ever, but as part of the deal it was sort of hidden under a blanket of a payment for restitution. Tom decided to call some of his prospective clients in the afternoon after this whole Schroller thing was wrapped up.

Just before nine, Marco walked in. He looked around from the Qing vase to the parcel sitting on a chair.

"Did the German call?"

"Haven't heard a thing yet. Just got in."

"I see you've got the package ready."

"Yeah, all wrapped up for delivery."

"Good," Marco said, taking a look at the vase.

"So, you're selling this piece. Is it really worth that much?"

"Better believe it. Depends also on who buys it of course."

"I guess I don't understand your business that well," Marco said shaking his head.

"Simple. In my business it's demand that drives the price."

"So, the document I bought was in high demand?" he asked, not able to resist the temptation to bring the fundamentals of his deal up again.

"As far as I knew it was the only copy," Tom answered testily.

"Okay, forget it. Anyway, what kind of vase did you say this was?" he asked, bending down to look at it more closely.

Tom was checking his phone and barely heard the question.

"A Qing, I mean a Ming vase," he lied.

"What's the difference?" Marco asked, raising his eyebrows.

"Oh, about 400 years and a factor of ten in pricing."

"So, which one is it?"

Tom was about to declare it a Ming, when his phone rang.

"Tom Ardens," he answered, then holding his hand over the phone, mouthed to Marco, "It's him."

Tom listened for a while then answered.

"Okay, I got it. I'll be there in an hour," he said, taking his jacket from his desk.

He turned to Marco after ending the call.

"He wants to meet at the amphitheater near Turtle Pond in Central Park. I think that's very close to the museum."

"I know where it is. It's a bit off the beaten path. Very few people around that area of the park. I know of a good lookout spot there where I can keep an eye on things."

"Hold on, he wants me to put the painting in a black garbage bag and put tape around it," Tom said, picking up the package.

Tom walked to the back room and found a bag, put the package in it and ran Scotch tape around it a few times.

"Let's go and collect a 100K," he said when he came back into the storefront.

"You mean, let's go get the perp, I assume?" Marco asked.

"Of course," Tom said. "I'll call you if I get any more instructions. Let's do this."

Tom locked up his office and walked to his car.

Marco got into in his own car and made a call.

"Detective O'Grady, please," he said to the station operator.

O'Grady was a seasoned detective who had been a partner of Marco's when he started out. At six feet two, he had a commanding presence and always seemed to get the most interesting cases. He had a square face with brown eyes and a perpetual smile. His curly hair was borderline red. Unshaven, his rusty beard gave him a tough look. He and Marco kept in touch the past few years. Marco had called him earlier in the day and he followed up on Marco's request.

"Hey, Marco," he said with a deep voice.

"Have you gotten anything on that car I called about?"

"It's a rental. The guy's name is probably an alias: Fritz Schroller. No legitimate or known address."

"Find out anything about him, in case that is his name?"

"Nothing yet, I have a guy on it."

"All right, thanks," Marco said and hung up.

Tom pulled off 79th Street Traverse toward the amphitheater on the side of Turtle Pond. He had no idea where Schroller wanted to meet, so he parked in front of a utility building. He walked passed the stage on the path that hugged the pond. At the north end of the pond near a few trees, he paused and put the package down. He checked his phone and waited.

Schroller had positioned himself near one of the baseball fields in the park with a good view of two access roads and the circular road around a treeless grassy area. With binoculars, he scanned from right to left, starting at the amphitheater. Noticing a police car, he followed it as it moved on behind the utility building and headed back for 79th Street. He noticed Tom coming in and stopping just past the theater. At the same time he caught a reflection of another car that drove by the park. He followed it until almost disappeared behind the other side of the theater, and then it suddenly stopped. He only saw part of the trunk. He was sure it was parked there because he could make out a bumper. There was no movement around the car. He checked on Tom who was standing still and then scanned back to the car but still saw nothing move. He considered the vehicle to be an unmarked police car and kept his eyes on it. After a few minutes, his patience was rewarded when a man was partly visible behind the car. Schroller zoomed in closer and vaguely saw a man with binoculars through the tree branches. He swore and pulled back behind a tree, still in a good position to see Tom.

Tom checked his phone again, expecting further instruction. He picked up the parcel and held it in front of him. He had a feeling Schroller was watching him, so he used that as a signal to tell Schroller he was ready. Looking around, he suddenly saw Marco but cast his gaze right away toward the baseball fields, not wanting to give Marco's position away. He put the parcel down again and checked his watch. Ten o'clock. Right on time he figured. His phone rang.

"I'm here," he said, looking for where Schroller was hiding.

"I see you. Now let's shake your guard dog," he snapped.

"I don't know what you're talking about. Do you have the money?" he asked, trying to play innocent.

"Don't worry. Just follow my directions. I'm keeping an eye on you," Schroller said, looking for the other man with the binoculars. He had temporarily lost him.

"I'm listening."

"Stay on the path until you get to the circular path. Take a right and keep walking. I'll call you."

Tom took the parcel and started walking. Marco followed Tom from a distance, hiding as much as possible behind shrubs and trees. Tom reached the circular path and kept walking. His phone rang again.

"Go to the right into the woods. Do you see the package in a black garbage bag near the tree, about 10 yards in?" Schroller asked, lowering his voice since Tom was within 200 feet of where he was standing. He looked again for the other man, but didn't see him. Although he was concerned about that, his plan included that option and he would fool Tom's tail.

"Yes, I see it," Tom said.

"Good," Schroller said. "Put the painting down next to it and take my package. Stay on the phone."

Tom walked over to the tree, left his parcel and took the other similar looking one.

"Is the money in this thing?" Tom asked, shaking the package.

"Yes, but I don't want you to open it yet. Here's what you need to do: head left toward the baseball fields and take my package with you. Walk across the first field. Keep this line open and I will tell you where to go next. My eyes are on you."

"Okay, easy enough," Tom said. He hoped Marco was watching and keeping an eye on the location of the dropped package.

Marco had moved closer along the pond and had seen Tom walk into a small stand of trees. Tom reappeared a few seconds later with the package and he followed. He called Tom on his cell to ask what had happened in the woods, but his call went straight to voice mail. He focused his binoculars on Tom and saw that he had his phone to his ear.

Schroller watched Tom walk away from the dropped parcel and his hiding spot. As long as that man kept following Tom with the package, his plan would work.

Marco had moved closer to the circular road and found it harder to stay out of sight. By making a loop around the open area behind several rows of trees, he actually had gotten closer to Schroller. He focused on Tom again who seemed to have backtracked with the package.

"Go to the one tree beyond the field. Open the package there," Schroller said to Tom and hung up. He left his hiding place and walked between the trees toward the package. He grabbed it and smiled while running through the woods to a parallel road behind the Met. He jumped into his parked car and sped off.

Marco had just lowered his binoculars as he heard a car behind him speeding away. Instinctively he knew that something was not right and ran toward the road he had come in on. He saw a black Mercedes on 79th Avenue Traverse going east, and swore. He ran for his car but already realized that Schroller would have a huge head start on him. Not exactly what he had planned. Out of breath, he opened his car door and called Tom, who had closed his phone when he didn't get any further instructions.

"Tom, don't you still have the painting? He's already taken off in his car!" he yelled.

"I picked up another package and I'm supposed to open it here. I left my package in the woods."

"Damn, I get it now. He wanted me to think you still had the painting."

"Are you following him?"

"I am just getting to the road, I don't see him now, but I'm assuming he's on 79th."

"Do you see his car?"

"No, not yet! I'm going to have to run a few lights here if I'm going to catch up with him."

"Okay, I'm running to my car. I'll be right behind you."

Marco stepped on it and in the distance he thought he saw the back of the black Mercedes. When he got to the next light it was red and every lane was blocked by waiting cars. He beat his fists on his steering wheel. There was no way for him to catch up with Schroller now. He called Tom again.

"Sorry, I've lost him. I'm calling the cops. They're nearby and can possibly stop him. They have the APB on his car."

"I thought we weren't bringing the police into this?" Tom asked surprised.

"Filing that B&E gave the police a justification to pick him up when they spotted him."

"At least they didn't show up here. You didn't tell them did you?"

"No, not yet."

"All right, don't sweat it. He's not going to be a happy camper anyway."

"What do you mean?"

"You didn't think I put the real painting in that package did you? He's got nothing but wood and newspaper," Tom laughed.

"What the hell? You're kidding me right? I'm risking my neck here, following this guy and all for a fake painting? You're a fool. Dammit. I can't believe this shit," Marco yelled.

"Hey, listen," Tom said, no longer laughing. "I wasn't about to walk in Central Park with a multi-million dollar painting."

"You should've been up front with me. See, that's what I don't like about you. You'll deceive anybody for your own advantage. Now you'll pay the price."

"What do you mean?"

"He's out 100K. Did you check the money?"

"I'll check it in a second. I'm at a red light."

Tom ripped the package open. All he saw was newspaper. He picked up his phone.

"Damn, no money. All we exchanged is old newspapers," Tom said, sounding disappointed.

"Forget the money. The guy is really pissed by now and he'll become bolder and more dangerous."

"Well, the way I see it, it's a good thing I didn't give him the painting. Have you caught up with him yet?"

"He's long gone now. I'm not chasing a bag of wood and paper. I'm stuck behind a garbage truck anyway."

"Are you still calling the cops?" Tom asked.

"Of course. They have a better chance than we do. Let's meet at your office."

"Fine with me, see you in about forty five minutes," Tom said and hung up.

At about the same time Marco and Tom were heading for the Midtown Tunnel, Schroller had backtracked in a big loop toward the Met. He parked his car and got out. He opened the back door and put the parcel flat on the back seat and stripped the brown paper away. Immediately he saw an empty frame with newspaper. He backed off and swore.

"*Gottverdammter Idiot! Scheisse!*" he yelled, as he grabbed all the material and threw it onto the sidewalk.

He got behind the wheel and leaned over to the glove compartment. He took out a .45 magnum and checked the ammo. He tucked the gun between his belt and the back of his shirt and covered it up with his jacket. He got out of his car and leaned up against the front hood facing the Met entrance. He lit up a cigarillo.

CHAPTER 21

Wednesday Noon

"MAN, I'M PISSED," Marco said as he walked into Tom's store.

Tom didn't respond right away and Marco continued.

"We were so close."

Tom was expecting a heap of criticism to come his way for having deceived Marco. On the way back to the store, he realized he should have told Marco that there was no painting in the package. Then again, it was all about catching Schroller and maybe collecting a 100K. He was relieved to hear Marco talking about having missed the German.

"Yeah. I really thought you had him. What do we do now?"

"Nothing," Marco said and sat down.

Tom thought that Marco was no longer worried about his deception, but Marco quickly put that idea to rest.

"I'm pissed at you Tom. If I'm going to help you, you have to be honest with me. No surprises and no crap like you pulled this morning. Understood?" he asked, raising his voice.

Tom got up and closed the door to the back office. In situations like this, being put on the spot, Tom became defensive and tried to explain the issue away.

"Yeah, I get it. But it worked this time, didn't it?" he quipped.

"You still should have told me about the fake package. Any more crap like this and I'm done. You pay what you owe me and that's it."

"It won't happen again, I swear. I just want to know what our next step should be. If the cops don't catch him, Schroller will just keep coming back at us."

"See, here you go again. You knew the guy's name and you didn't tell me."

"You never asked and I didn't think of it. I would have told you."

"Whatever. I talked to some of my ex-colleagues at the precinct and . . ." Marco said, more relaxed as Tom interrupted him.

"I thought we weren't going to involve the police," he said.

"Hold on. Let me finish," Marco said calmly putting up his hands as if to ward Tom off. "All I asked them was to put an APB out like I told you. From the license plate they found out it was a rental for a guy named Fritz Schroller. The cops will track the guy for us. You and I will work with them to keep the guy away until after the auction."

"Okay then," Tom said, sitting back down. "I hope they find him. What can we do in the meantime?"

"We wait to hear something from the police. I'm hungry. Let's get some lunch at Dino's diner up the street."

The diner was one of the more unassuming restaurants in Queens. The original 60's diner had been remodeled with a brick wall as a fake façade, and a roof. It looked like any other single story building on the street. There was nothing left that showed the stainless steel hull from when the diner was first built. The back of the diner was pushed out to add a longer kitchen. On the inside, however, it had remained pretty much as it was more than forty years ago. Red was the predominant color of the wall decorations, covers of stools, chairs and booth seats. The counter and table tops were white Formica with plenty of cuts and coffee stains. The current cook had a reputation of making the best hamburgers around.

Marco ordered a medium rare with Swiss cheese and Tom wanted a Reuben with fries. While they were waiting for their food, Marco took a sip of his beer and continued their conversation.

"So, yesterday I talked to you about not paying me from another bogus deal."

"I heard you. The painting is obviously legit and the curator at the Met can vouch for it."

"How about that statue you just packed up at your store? Where did you get it?"

"Bought it from another dealer. It's Babylonian. Very valuable," Tom answered.

"Do you have papers on it?"

"A certificate. That's a guarantee."

"Okay, listen. I really hope you can cash in on your painting. Now, you've made some shady deals in the past. You've got to stop doing that. Your father wouldn't have liked that. This is your opportunity to fix things. So, stop running your business that way. Others like me will be on to you. They'll come after you. Capice?"

"Hey," Tom said. "Stop hammering at my business. I get it. Back to Schroller. So he's German?"

"That we don't know. Sounds German. Someone at the precinct is checking it out."

"Good. I hope they get him soon. They'll call you when they have anything, right?" Tom asked.

"Count on it," Marco said as the waitress brought their food.

CHAPTER 22

Wednesday Afternoon

ISABELLE HAD BEEN working at the Metropolitan Museum for four years. In her function as coordinator of special exhibitions in American 19th century art, she had gotten to know all the key people in the museum, especially the directors and the curators. She'd been offered jobs at other prestigious museums in the country, but nothing could compare to the exciting work at the Met. She had received her Master's Degree in Art History from Binghamton University in upstate New York. Having grown up in Valley Stream, Long Island, she had been keen to move to the city after she graduated. Her degree had prepared her well, but the last years had taught her so much more, having had access to the art work and the guidance of the curators. She had been so busy that she had decided to postpone getting her additional Master's in Museum Studies. She needed it to move into a curator position, however, she was content for now. She was heavily involved in coordinating an exhibition of paintings by Martin Johnson Heade. She was finishing up some desk work when Dr. Amado walked in.

"Hi, Isabelle. I've been trying to find Tom. Do you have any other phone numbers besides his cell?"

"Have you tried his store number?"

"Yes, I tried that also. Maybe he's at home?"

"He doesn't have a land line there, but I can give him a message if you'd like. I'll see him later."

"Thanks. I just wanted him to know that the Dutch expert is almost finished. He's excited and on the phone constantly to Holland. I don't know what he's saying, but I think Tom may have a winner here."

"That's great news!" Isabelle said, getting up. "I'm leaving for a late lunch. I'll be sure to keep trying him. Thanks."

"Good. Have him give me a call. I'm calling Metzer at Sotheby's in a few minutes and provide him with an update as well," Dr. Amado said, leaving her office.

Isabelle straightened a pile of papers on her desk, turned off her PC and closed her office. When she got off the elevator on the ground floor, she waved at a docent who was with a group of visitors. Very few people were in line at the security checkpoint in the lobby and she exited quickly through the main doors onto Fifth Avenue.

Schroller had been staring at the entrance for a long time now and smiled when he saw Isabelle appear. He took his jacket off and hung it over his left arm. He put his gun in his left hand and covered it with his jacket. He crossed the street and in no time he came up behind Isabelle. She was startled when he put his right arm around her shoulders.

"Hey, what . . ." she started to say and then recognized Schroller. "You! Leave me alone!" She tried to pull away from his arm, but Schroller had swung his left arm in front of him with the gun poking into her side.

"Shut up woman. Keep walking. Yes, that's a gun," he said firmly, keeping a smile on his face. Anyone walking by would recognize them as a couple and that's what Schroller wanted. Attracting attention to himself could potentially spoil his plans at another shot at getting the painting. Isabelle also realized that any fight at this point would endanger her life. She angrily turned to Schroller.

"What do you want from me?"

"Shut up. We're turning around and going back to the museum. If you try anything, you won't make your next meeting. Understand?"

Isabelle did not reply and followed Schroller's lead in making a U-turn on the sidewalk. He pulled her closer to him and she felt the gun barrel through her jacket poking her lower ribs.

"Now, we're going in through the side entrance using your access card. I don't want to even see the security checkpoint."

Having been told to shut up twice, Isabelle was hesitant to say anything, yet her best chance of getting away from Schroller was to stay very visible in the Met building where people would recognize her.

"There are cameras everywhere. They'll see you," she hissed quietly.

"Take the side entrance like I said," Schroller insisted as he pushed her passed the main entrance toward the loading dock area on the next street to the right.

She needed him to understand that he didn't have a chance to get what he wanted.

"You won't get away with this," she warned him.

"For the last time, shut up," Schroller said as they arrived at the side entrance.

Isabelle used her access card to enter the building. She knew that there would be a record somewhere of her entry, not that it would help her right now, but perhaps there was a guard monitoring this door through the outside camera. She was a little disappointed that no alarms went off.

Once inside, Schroller pushed Isabelle to the only door he saw. It was locked and needed an electronic card. Isabelle swiped her card and they entered a short hallway with several doors and stairs at the end.

"We'll take these stairs to the second floor," Schroller said, pushing Isabelle out in front of him.

"This will only get us in the exhibition rooms," she offered, not that she objected to that because there would be guards. As far as she knew they were not armed though. Schroller didn't mind as long as he kept her close to him. His objective was a special room.

"No problem. We're going to the restoration room."

"I don't have access to that," Isabelle replied, wondering how he knew where the room was.

"I'll make sure you do," he whispered confidently as he pushed Isabelle into the first exhibition room, making sure he had his right arm around her waist and the gun planted firmly into her side.

Almost immediately, an unarmed security guard recognized Isabelle as they walked by him. He smiled and nodded.

"Hi Isabelle, how's it going?" he asked.

Schroller didn't want her to get involved in any pleasantries that could delay his mission and pulled her a little closer to him.

"Smile and say 'fine' and keep walking," he said quietly through clenched teeth, trying to keep smiling at the same time.

Isabelle turned to the security guard.

"Fine. Thanks," she said briefly, moving on in the direction Schroller was pushing her.

The security guard smiled back and wandered away.

They passed the double room Schroller had been hiding in, when he was listening to the conversation between Dr. Amado, Dr. Stockton and that other man. The doors were open and Schroller quickly glanced inside. Nobody was in there. He stopped at the end of the hallway. To his left he saw the same door he had seen the men go in the day before.

"You need to open that door," he said.

"It's locked and my card does not work here," she said and briefly glanced over her shoulder. She saw that the guard had followed them slowly, seemingly uninterested and he was about ten yards back.

"Who has a key to it?" Schroller asked impatiently.

"A few guards."

The guard spotted them standing near the end of the hallway. It seemed like Isabelle and the man were having an argument. As he approached them, Schroller turned around slowly, increasing the pressure of the gun. The guard's demeanor had not changed. He was still smiling, directing his attention to Isabelle.

"May I help you with something, Isabelle?"

"You don't have a key to that door, do you?" Isabelle asked, and, as Schroller took his eyes off her looking at the guard for a response, she slightly shook her head. Noticing that the guard suddenly had a quizzical look on his face, she moved her head a few times in the direction of Schroller's jacket at her side. Schroller however, had seen the look on the guard's face and immediately suspected something was wrong. He saw the guard quickly trip a silent alarm by touching a button on the wall. He had no choice. He pulled his gun away from Isabelle and pointed it at the security guard.

"Well, do you have a key or not?" he demanded.

"No, and let her go," the guard said, quickly raising his hands. "There's no way out of here."

When Schroller didn't answer right away, the guard, still more than twenty feet away, lowered his arms and pushed the *talk* button on his microphone and dove into the door opening of the large room. Immediately Schroller fired at him and missed. The guard got up and closed the door, calling for armed backup. Schroller knew that time was of the essence. Still holding on to Isabelle's arm with his right hand, he jerked her around toward the locked door and fired several bullets into the lock. If the first shot didn't cause consternation and panic in the exhibition room, with people standing frozen in place, the chaos now was complete. Some patrons actually started running toward them in the direction of an exit sign, but then quickly backtracked to the exhibition rooms. Most people headed for the stairs. The shrieking and screaming annoyed Schroller, so to clear the room, he fired a few shots into the exhibition room just as two armed security men entered. As they dived behind a free standing wall, Schroller tried the door handle. The door didn't budge and he realized that he wasn't going to get anywhere. He fired two more bullets into the lock, but the door remained locked. He quickly pointed his gun at Isabelle's head when he saw the guards come out of hiding aiming their guns at him.

"Back off," he yelled, but they kept their guns drawn and ready.

Schroller used Isabelle as a shield and forced her back to the stairs, walking backwards to the door, keeping the gun at her head and his eyes on the guards.

"You follow us down the stairs and she's dead," he yelled at them as he pushed the door open.

The guards ran for the door when Schroller and Isabelle disappeared, but a volley of bullets kept them from entering the stairwell. The unarmed guard had asked for help on the ground floor, expecting Schroller and Isabelle to appear in the lobby. Running down the stairs quickly toward the short hallway, Schroller stopped and pointed at a door different than the one that lead to the side access door.

"What's behind this door?" he asked, twisting her arm behind her back.

"That's the loading dock," Isabelle said, trembling and scared.

"Open the door," he demanded.

Isabelle opened the door with her card and they entered the loading dock area. There was nobody around and Schroller dragged Isabelle across the room toward a door with a standard *EXIT* sign above it. He put his jacket back over his left arm with his gun in position and his right arm around Isabelle's waist. He leaned into the horizontal handle on the door, pushed it open, and they stepped outside. He then calmly directed her to Fifth Avenue where they disappeared into the crowd. Sirens seemed to converge from every direction behind them. As they crossed the street toward his car, Schroller looked over his shoulder and saw police cars and several cops, guns drawn, run up the steps into the museum. Isabelle realized that they wouldn't see her and started to yell, but having gotten to his car, Schroller quickly opened it and forced Isabelle in through the driver's side, keeping his gun pointed at her the whole time. She climbed over the shift stick and for a second contemplated running out the passenger door, but she felt the gun in her back as Schroller got into the car. She couldn't believe that nobody paid any attention to them. Everyone was looking directly at the mayhem in front of the museum, unaware of the fact that she was being kidnapped. Schroller started the engine and looked in his rear view mirror. More police cars were driving up behind him, while he slowly pulled away from the museum.

"I'll get that painting yet. Your boyfriend will be happy to give it to me soon," he said, very pissed that he had failed again.

CHAPTER 23

Wednesday Late Afternoon

MARCO WAS DRIVING through Queens and had just gotten off the phone with O'Grady. He pushed the number for Tom who answered almost immediately.

"Tom, listen. There may be a problem. Someone tried to get access to the offices at the Met. Shots were fired but nobody's injured. Apparently someone took a hostage and left the building. It's a mess over there."

Tom was driving back from a visit to a prospective client and had just turned his phone on when Marco called.

"Really, do they know who it was?"

"I just heard on the radio that it was a man trying to break into the offices."

"You're fucking kidding me, right? Could this be Schroller? Let me call Isabelle, she'll know what went on. Hold on," Tom said all agitated, putting Marco on hold and dialing Isabelle.

Isabelle's phone kept ringing so he switched back to Marco.

"Marco, hey, she's not answering. She's probably in a meeting about what happened. I'll try her later."

"Hold on Tom, I got another call," Marco said, looking at the number displayed on his phone. "It's the precinct, hold on."

Marco listened, and went back to Tom.

"Good news, Tom! Schroller's car was reported seen at a motel in Queens. The manager called in when he saw the APB on TV."

"Are the cops picking him up? They can arrest him on the breaking and entering, right?"

"They'll dispatch a unit," Marco assured him.

"Why don't we go there? I want to be there when they pick him up."

"Easy, Tom. This is a job for the police," Marco said.

"C'mon, I want to go. Maybe we can even bust the guy before the cops get there."

"Not so fast Rambo. All we can do is to stake out the place and if we see him, we'll keep an eye on him until the cops get there," Marco said.

"All right. Which motel?"

"The Red Roof Inn on 54ᵗʰ," Marco sighed.

"See you in the lobby in five minutes," Tom said and stepped on the gas.

Inside a motel room in Queens, not far from the expressway, Schroller was tying up Isabelle to one of the beds. The room reeked of cigar smoke, and the ashtray was full of cigarillo stubs. Her wrists were tied together in front of her and he raised them above her head until they were touching the post of the headboard. Isabelle felt her rib cage being twisted and cried out in pain. Schroller told her to shut up and tied her wrists tightly to the knob on top of the post. She was sitting up with her back against the headboard and her right arm extended across her face. For good measure, he tied her ankles together not caring whether she was uncomfortable in that position or not. He went into the bathroom and returned with a washcloth which he promptly stuck in her mouth. Almost immediately Isabelle gagged, but after breathing through her nose for a few seconds she calmed down and brought her breathing under control.

Schroller lit another cigarillo and turned on the TV.

Tom parked his car near the entrance of the Red Roof Inn and quickly got out. He ran for the entrance and pushed the door open with both hands. Marco was already standing at the registration counter, waiting for the manager.

"Do you know what room he's in?" Tom asked, eager to find Schroller.

"Hold on," Marco said as the manager appeared.

"Yes, can I help you?"

"I'm detective Vincente," Marco said, flashing an old badge. "You called about the car?"

"Yeah, that guest is in 152, but I haven't seen the car today."

"He was here yesterday?"

"I think so. By the way, he's paid for the room in advance for five days," the manager volunteered.

"Thanks. We want to take a quick look in his room. May we have a key?"

The manager shrugged his shoulders, grabbed a key from a hook on the wall and handed it over.

"Don't forget to bring it back."

Once outside, Marco looked left and right.

"I'm surprised the unit isn't here yet. We have the key so we saved them some time. Let's keep an eye on the room."

Tom nodded and they walked through the parking lot until they could see the room number on a door. There were no cars parked in front, and a quick scan by Marco confirmed what the manager had said.

"His car isn't here, at least I don't see it."

"So, why don't we check out the room anyway?"

"Let's wait here," Marco answered. "The police will be here any second."

"Honestly, I don't think he's here. So, what's stopping us?"

"He could be hiding his car somewhere else. He's got a gun and I don't want to walk in on something," Marco said.

"You could knock on the door. He doesn't know you. You could say you have the wrong room and walk away. Then the cops can take care of the rest," Tom offered.

After waiting a few more minutes, Marco decided that he could indeed check out whether anyone was in the room.

"Stay here until I call you," he said to Tom, and walked to the door. He knocked and got no answer. He knocked again and looked through an opening in the curtain into the room. The lights were out and no sound came from the room. He decided to go in so he unlocked the door. As he pushed it slowly open, he kept saying *Hello*, waiting for a response. When none came, he swung the door wide open, holding his gun to his side. The room was empty. He saw a bed that was made up, and didn't notice any suitcases or personal things.

Marco stepped back outside after turning the light on and motioned for Tom to come.

"It doesn't look like anyone's staying here," Marco said.

"That's strange, why would he pay for several days and not even stay here. Let me check the bathroom."

Tom walked into the bathroom and besides the small shampoo bottle, rinse and a small unwrapped bar of soap, nothing else was in the bathroom.

"Nah, it's empty. Do we have the right room?" he asked.

Marco turned around, and with the handkerchief he picked up a brown stub and held it up.

"Oh yeah we do. That's a cigarillo stub. He was here."

Tom spotted a USA Today on the small table underneath a hotel guide book.

"This is Monday's edition. I don't think he's been here in two days. What do you make of it?

"This place is a decoy. He's not coming back here. There are no clothes or a suitcase."

"Damn, we have to keep looking," Tom said.

Marco was about to say something when two policemen knocked on the door.

"Heard you were already here, detective," one of them said.

"There's nobody staying here. It's a decoy."

"Okay, sir," the policeman said. "We'll be on our way then." He called his report in to the station as they left.

Marco looked one more time around, and shook his head.

"So, Schroller's staying somewhere else. Too many motels here to check, but they'll get him. Don't worry. Let's go."

"Okay, keep me posted. Did you hear anything more about that thing at the Met?"

"No, but I'm sure the captain will call me if it's important. I'll call you later. I'm taking the key back now," he said, walking away toward the lobby.

Tom walked to his car and started it. Before he drove off, he called Isabelle's cell and he got her voicemail this time.

"Hey, Izzy. Been trying to reach you today. Must be a long meeting. Heard about the happenings at the Met. Hope everything's calm there now. Call me. Maybe I can come into the city again tonight and we'll go to that Brasserie place."

Driving to his office, Tom thought about his encounters with Schroller. The first time, he offered him money for the painting. It still puzzled Tom how Schroller knew he had the painting and where he lived. He must have been on to him for a while, he figured. The second time, he entered his apartment. Neither Tom nor Marco had been able to figure how he got in, but that didn't matter as much as how traumatizing it was for them, especially Isabelle. Then there was the exchange at the park. It was likely that Schroller didn't have the money at all, unless he expected a dummy package. He realized he didn't see Schroller then, but in talking with him on the phone, it sounded more like he was trying to outsmart him. He was sure that Schroller couldn't possibly expect him to just turn over that painting. So why had they gone through the whole charade?

Tom was about to park in front of his store when it hit him. What had Schroller said just before he left their bedroom? What was it again, *Delivery or Take-out* or something like that? Tom figured it out. He slammed his hand on the steering wheel, abruptly stepped on the gas and made a U-turn, driving as fast as he could to Isabelle's place in Brooklyn. He had a sudden uncomfortable feeling and when a few more calls to her office number and her cell phone were unanswered, he started to panic. Within fifteen minutes he arrived at her building.

In the foyer he rang her apartment bell again and again, and still there was no answer. Just when he was about to call Dr. Amado at the Met, another tenant walked into the foyer.

"Hi, my name is Tom. I'm Isabelle's boyfriend, and . . ." he said to the woman, who interrupted him.

"I know who you are, young man. I've seen you here before. As for Isabelle, I think she's at work," she said.

"That's the problem. She's not answering her phone at work or her cell phone, so I was worried."

The woman opened the door to the stairwell and smiled.

"Go ahead and check."

Tom flew up the stairs to the second floor, yelling *Thank you* half way up. He took a deep breath and knocked on Isabelle's apartment door. There was no answer. The elevator door opened and the woman got off.

"I told you she wasn't in," she said right away, shaking her head.

"Have you seen her at all today?" he asked.

"Sorry, she left early this morning and sometimes I see her at night when she comes in, but no, I haven't seen her today," she said, ready to open her own apartment door.

"Thanks," Tom mumbled and dashed down the stairs again.

In the motel room, Schroller checked Isabelle and made sure she was tied properly to the bed. He took the cloth out of her mouth. Before he could put tape over it, she yelled at him.

"Untie my hands! I can hardly feel them in this position."

Schroller didn't answer and while Isabelle protested and shook her head, he forced the tape over her mouth. He locked the room on his way out, drove for about five miles and parked the car. He took his phone and dialed a number in Germany.

At the house in Düsseldorf, the German father and son were sitting at a table. The son recognized the number and pushed the *speaker* button.

"Hallo, Fritz," he said.

"Guten Abend," Schroller said.

"Any progress?" the old man asked.

"I took the man's girlfriend today. He will trade the painting soon."

The old man had a puzzled look on his face, turned to his son and then to the phone.

"You have a hostage?"

"Don't worry, this will be easy," Schroller said, laughing

"Put the screws on if he won't give you the painting tomorrow," the son said.

"I know what to do."

"Listen, I don't want anyone killed," the old man said, leaning over the phone.

"Don't worry, old man. Tonight I will have my second hostage," Schroller announced.

"Who's that?" the son asked.

"Let me just say that by morning, the painting will be worthless and easy to give up," Schroller assured them.

"Better make sure of that quickly before the police find you."

"All is going according to plan."

"How about the boyfriend? Have you demanded the painting for the girlfriend yet?" the son asked.

"No, not yet. He's not a threat. He does have someone helping him out, but obviously not a professional. No, this will be easy."

"Good then. Call us when you have the Rembrandt," the old man said, raising his eyebrows. The son hung up the phone.

CHAPTER 24

Wednesday Early Evening

TOM WAS DRIVING back to his apartment. There was a chance Isabelle had gone there and that there was something wrong with her phone. If she wasn't there he'd drive downtown to the Met. He had called Dr. Amado at the Met, but apparently he was in a meeting. Maybe Marco knew something more by now, he thought, and called.

"Marco, I went over to Isabelle's place and she's not there. Something's wrong. I'm on my way to my place and if she's not there, I'm off to the Met."

"Oh? What are you thinking?"

"What if she's the one that was kidnapped?"

"What? I hope not. Call me if she's not at your apartment and I'll meet you at the Met."

Tom didn't spend much time at his apartment since Isabelle wasn't there. He drove to the Long Island Expressway and headed for the city. He called Marco to tell him he was heading for the Met.

It was getting dark by the time he parked near the museum. Inside he asked for Isabelle, but the guard at the desk could not get an answer.

"Could you call Dr. Amado for me," he asked, wiping his forehead.

The guard called and handed the phone to Tom.

"Dr. Amado? It's Tom Arden," Tom said anxiously.

"Tom, I've been trying to reach you for a while. Please come on up to the third floor. Someone will come and get you at the elevator. We're in the security room," he said, hanging up.

Tom told the guard what Dr. Amado said and he walked to the elevator and waited. When the door opened a guard motioned him inside and they went up in the elevator. Tom's heart was racing ever since he had talked to Dr. Amado. The man knew something and wasn't telling him. By the time he was shown into the security room, he was very nervous and could only think that this was about Isabelle.

Dr. Amado greeted him and introduced him to the Met's security officer, Mike, who didn't waste any time.

"We've been reviewing the tapes here."

"And? What did you see? Is it Isabelle?" Tom asked looking from the screen to Dr. Amado and back to the monitor.

"You're the young woman's friend, right?" Mike asked.

"Isabelle. Yes, why . . . ?" Tom asked, but Dr. Amado interrupted.

"Tom, I'm really sorry to have to tell you, but Isabelle has been kidnapped by . . ."

"Dammit, I knew it! Show me the recording," he said.

"I was about to," Mike said as he reset the DVR recording.

They watched for a few moments.

"One of our guards saw her with the kidnapper. We know they left through the loading dock. That's on another disk."

Tom looked closely at the picture of Isabelle with a man at her side. At one point, the man turned slightly and Tom recognized him immediately.

"It's the German! It's Schroller!" Tom yelled just as Marco walked in.

"Gentlemen, detective Vincente. What's that about Schroller?" Marco asked.

"He's kidnapped Isabelle. Look, he's got her pulled close to him," Tom said pointing at the picture showing Schroller and Isabelle just as they were leaving toward the stairwell.

"Do you have other DVD recordings from that area?" Marco asked.

"We have the loading dock area coming right up," Mike said and worked the keyboard.

Marco turned to Tom and put his hand on his shoulder.

"Man, I'm sorry. This changes everything. This is something for the police."

"Oh, they've already been here and seen this. They uploaded all our DVR content to their server. You can check with them to see what's happening. The officer in charge is O'Grady," Dr. Amado said.

"Right. I know him. We'll head over there right now," Marco said.

"Before you go, I want you to know, Tom, that Mr. van Weteren has just about declared the painting a true Rembrandt. I was trying to reach you around lunch time to tell you that, but with all that's happened since then, it almost slipped my mind," Dr. Amado said.

Tom's face lit up for a few moments.

"That's great. I was counting on that," was all he could say, his thoughts on Isabelle.

"I'm sure we'll get the same confirmation from Dr. Stockton," Dr. Amado said. "But first, let's get Isabelle back."

Tom and Marco had left the security room after thanking Dr. Amado. They were in the elevator.

"Listen Tom, it's decision time. You know what Schroller wants and this time it will have to be the real painting," Marco said.

"Yes, I'm well aware of that. What do you think of offering him money first?" Tom asked, having thought about the predicament he was in now.

"Be serious. He's the one who wanted to give *you* money. You can't pay a guy like that off. The ransom won't be money, it will be the Rembrandt. You've got no choice."

"Yes, I do," Tom said stubbornly as they walked through the lobby. "It may be my painting now, but by Friday afternoon, someone else may own it and what good is Isabelle to him then?"

"What are you saying? You want Isabelle in Schroller's hands for two days? And then what?"

"I want to explain that to the police. How well do you know that O'Grady?"

"Good luck telling them that. O'Grady was an up and coming guy when I was finishing up. He's good, and he knows about your mess with Schroller already. Anyway, I'll wait up front in my car. Follow me in yours to the precinct.

CHAPTER 25

Wednesday Evening

TOM AND MARCO had returned to Tom's apartment after their visit with O'Grady. It was clear that the police were in charge now, but they had no leads to go on. They had suggested Marco stay with Tom for a while until they could relieve him later with a kidnapping task unit. They wanted to be there to handle the ransom call. O'Grady had warned that it was possible that they might not hear anything that night, but given the situation, there was some urgency for Schroller to get the ransom before the auction.

Tom was in the bedroom when his phone rang. He saw that it was an 800 number. He moved his finger across *Slide to Unlock* to take the call.

"This is a courtesy call from Citibank Credit. We did not . . ." a female voice said. Tom hung up walked to the kitchen.

While Marco was draining spaghetti, Tom sat down at the kitchen table, tapping his fingers. There was a salad on the table and Marco stirred the sauce on the gas stove.

"Thanks for coming over and doing the cooking," Tom said.

"No problem. A good meal will do you good."

"Yeah, I know. That briefing at the police station got me all jittery. I don't have a good feeling about that O'Grady guy."

"Hey, he's got the whole force looking for her. Things will start happening once Schroller demands the ransom. Let the police do their work. I know you want to help but that's not your job."

Tom leaned back on the chair, admiring Marco's kitchen skills.

"I guess not. Anyway, where did you learn how to cook?"

"At home first, helping my mother, but later, after twenty five years of marriage, my wife announced that she'd had enough kitchen time. Your turn," she said."

"Well, it smells good. I can't even get a can of soup right. This salad is about the extent of my culinary exploits."

"No problem. Happy to do it. Is your phone on and charged?"

"I just checked. I'm ready, and nervous."

"You know what he wants. There's no secret there Tom."

"Don't I fucking know! Not sure what I'm going to do though . . ."

Marco put the pots on the table and started serving.

"What do you mean? It's simple. The painting for Isabelle. It's the only way. The police's job will be to get him before he gets too far with the painting."

"Well, I hope they do better than we did at the park with the fake painting. I'm not so sure. What if the cops fuck this up?"

"Have some faith, man. They'll take care of the bastard. What's important is that Isabelle is safe and set free."

Marco finished serving and sat down, sprinkling parmesan cheese on his bowl of pasta and meat sauce.

"Let's eat."

After a few bites, Tom rested his spoon and fork on the side of his plate and looked up at Marco.

"I was thinking. The auction is still scheduled for Friday. If I stall him on the exchange of painting, he'll have to come to the auction. That's his last chance."

"C'mon, that's bullshit. Schroller will kill her because he'll be pissed off. Then he'll target whoever owns the painting after the auction. He's more ruthless than you know."

"Well, can't we at least lure him to the auction by stalling?"

"I wouldn't bet on it," Marco said, continuing to eat.

Tom dug into his spaghetti again and it was quiet for a few moments. They both jumped when Tom's iPhone, lying on the table, suddenly buzzed. Tom reached over and saw he had a message.

"Isabelle for painting, or else. Further instructions tomorrow," he read aloud and put the phone back down on the table.

"Well, that confirms it. Nothing we can do unless the APB turns up another lead," Marco said, getting his own phone from its hip clip.

"Are you calling O'Grady?"

"Already ringing," Marco said, shoving his chair back from the table. Tom had stepped outside onto the small balcony. He took a deep breath and walked back in, shaking his head, just as Marco finished his call.

"They traced the text message through AT&T already. It came from the New Rochelle area from an unregistered phone. The local cops are already checking motels in the area."

"What can we do?"

"You could call Amado and tell him to get the painting ready for you to pick up tomorrow morning."

"I don't think I can hand over the painting. I'll be ruined."

"You're fucking killing me, man. I can't believe you just said that. Your girlfriend is kidnapped and you can get her back easily and all I hear you talk about is the stupid painting."

"You know how much that painting is worth! The way I see it, in two days it's all over and, like I said, Isabelle wouldn't matter to him anymore," Tom said.

"You're missing the point. The essential words in his message are *or else*. If he doesn't get the painting, Isabelle may not make it," Marco said firmly. Having lost his appetite he started clearing the table. Tom was tapping his fingers again, staring at the floor.

"You know, I thought I had all my problems taken care of. The bank will foreclose on the store. I'll lose my entire inventory because I used it as collateral. I'll be kicked out of this apartment. Finding that painting was the best thing that has ever happened to me. The painting is my ticket out of a deep, deep hole," Tom said with a dejected voice.

"So, before you found that painting you were trying to get money how?" Marco asked, turning from the counter to Tom.

"Selling the stuff in my store."

"At highly inflated prices, I assume," Marco said, drying his hands and leaning against the counter.

"There's no other way."

"Probably sold some fake stuff too, huh?"

"Yeah, so what?"

"It's the principle of the thing."

"Fuck principle! Who gives a shit? If some simpleton wants to buy something so badly, I fill the need."

"That's what I am, right?"

"You know what I mean."

"No, I don't. You explain it to me."

"You got a real piece and paid top dollar for it. End of story."

"All right, but what about the next guy?"

"What next guy?"

"The one who wants the vase or the one who wants the statue."

"Suckers," Tom sneered and stood up.

"See what I mean. I bet you, the vase is probably a knock-off."

"Not quite, it's just a different dynasty, but the guy is researching it, so instead of making sixty thousand I'll make only a few thousand."

"That sounds a lot more honest and fair."

"Yeah, who cares," Tom said, putting dishes in the sink.

"How about that statue? Babylonian, you said? Marco asked, picking up his jacket from a chair in the living room.

"It's genuine."

"Would it surprise you that I happen to know it was looted from the Baghdad Museum at the beginning of the Iraq war?"

"How do you know that?"

"Aha! You admit it."

"Who told you?"

"Nobody. I just looked some things up."

Tom looked away and was quiet while Marco put on his jacket, put his phone in his pocket and walked to the apartment door.

"I'm telling you, it's time for you to set things right. With me, and with others. Go and see someone at the bank and tell them about the painting. They may give you some more time. It's all up to you. And another thing, go get that damn painting first thing in the morning!"

Marco slammed the door shut behind him. Tom sat down again and covered his face as he planted his elbows on the table. After a few moments, he got up, grabbed his jacket and left.

Tom drove from one motel to the next, showing a picture of Isabelle, asking motel managers whether they had seen her. He struck out at every single location and as the evening wore on, he got more and more frustrated. Finally, he gave up and headed back to his apartment.

Schroller returned to the motel room and turned on the light, briefly blinding Isabelle. He walked over to her and ripped the tape off her mouth.

"Ouch," Isabelle said but Schroller didn't react to her. He sat on the other bed facing her.

"Your boyfriend now has an easy task. He brings me the painting and you're free."

"Please let my arms down! I can't feel my fingers anymore," Isabelle begged.

Schroller untied her bound wrists from the bedpost.

"Here you go," Schroller said. "We wouldn't want these beautiful arms to go numb."

"What do you want with that painting anyway? If there's a legitimate claim to it, why don't those people come forward?" she asked.

"This painting belongs to a very important family in Germany. They are the rightful owners. I even offered your boyfriend money for it, but no, he likes playing games."

"Tom knows what he's doing. And that painting cannot possibly belong to that family. Unless they are from the House of Orange, but that's not likely."

"But of course they are. They had the painting for a hundred years, so you can imagine that they want it back."

Isabelle knew he was lying since her research had shown that there was no link with the House of Orange left in Germany. That branch had died out. How that family got it after it disappeared, she didn't know, but surely, they had no valid claim. That painting disappeared more than 250 years ago. She decided to press him a little on what he really knew.

"A hundred years?"

"Makes a good case, no?"

"If they can claim it, as you say, why don't they just contact the Metropolitan Museum? Kidnapping me doesn't help their case."

"But it does, you see. They don't want anyone to know they have such a valuable masterpiece, and they told me to use any means to get it."

"Think about it, rightful owners wouldn't do that."

Schroller was getting enough of all the questions and had checked his watch a few times already.

"It was stolen from them and they have been through a lot. The family wants to handle all of this discreetly. Anyway, as I said, Tom has an easy task now."

"Just let me go," Isabelle tried. "I will let the curator at the Met know about the German family. I'm sure they can work it all out."

Schroller laughed out loud.

"Really?" he asked. "They are true Germans and they don't trust Americans."

"Let me make a call," Isabelle said. "I can straighten this all out."

"You don't need to straighten anything out," Schroller said, getting up. "I do best when I stick to my own plan."

"So, how much are you being paid for all this criminal activity?" Isabelle asked when she saw Schroller reach for the tape again.

"More than you or your boyfriend could ever pay me," he said and pulled a piece of tape off and put it over Isabelle's mouth. He then tied her bound wrists to a lower position on the post.

"You know, I am going to make it even easier for Tom to part with the painting. You'll see. Get some sleep. Don't wait up for me. I'll be back late," he said.

He checked his .45 and tucked it away against his lower back. He put on his jacket and left, hanging the *Do not Disturb* sign on the outside door again.

CHAPTER 26

Wednesday Late Evening

TRAFFIC WAS STILL dense on the way into the city, but Schroller wasn't in a hurry. Isabelle was safely locked up and his next target was a bit of a hit or miss. If he succeeded it would be the extra insurance he needed to get the painting without much additional effort. He knew people would do anything to get loved ones back. If the police would stay out of things, cases could get resolved very quickly and have happy endings for everyone. It all depended on the ransom of course. Isabelle could serve well as a way to fetch a lot of money, but this painting was worth millions. His recent experience with this Tom character had taken him aback a little. Not only did he play games and think he could outsmart a German like himself, but he might actually balk at the ransom until after the auction. He could not risk that happening because it would change all the parameters. He would have to deal with different people or even a corporation then. No! Immediate and firm pressure was needed to pull this off before the painting went to auction.

At this time of evening, driving in Manhattan was much easier with mostly only cabs and limos to worry about. He had to find his way using the Tom-Tom GPS he had brought along. He followed the instructions in German and his mind drifted again to the situation he had created. He had to put pressure on Tom, no doubt, because there were less than 48 hours left. With a bit of luck, he could reduce the value of the painting to a few thousand dollars, thereby making it easier to give it up. If Tom delayed again, there would be another, simpler method to make Tom give him the painting. Isabelle seemed like the perfect girl to use for that.

He worked his way to 78th street and drove a little slower, looking for a sign for one of the properties of New York University. After a few minutes he found the Conservation Center. He parked across the street and looked at his watch. It was nearly 11 p.m. There were several lights on in offices on the second floor. He lit a cigarillo once outside of his car and leaned against the door, staring at the bright windows across the street.

Within ten minutes, a room suddenly went dark and Schroller crossed the street. He walked to the bottom steps of the entrance. Someone turned a light on in the hallway and he threw his cigarillo on the ground, crushing it with his heel. The ornate wrought iron door opened and a young man exited. Schroller greeted him briefly, slipping inside before the heavy and slowly closing door fell shut. Inside, he looked at a directory of departments and found that Curatorial Studies was on the second floor. He adjusted his gun in his belt and walked up the broad stairway.

Dr. Stockton was standing and staring at a large screen on a wall of his lab. He looked down and typed something, then checked another monitor before writing down something in a notebook. The large screen showed a super enlarged section of a painting, and a multitude of changing numbers that flashed at regular intervals. Dr. Stockton moved a stylus over a section of the screen and new numbers appeared next to brushstrokes. Some numbers hovered over the beginnings and ends of long strokes in pre-defined rectangles representing less than a square centimeter. One number in a large font in the top right corner kept increasing slowly until it finally settled at 96%.

Dr. Stockton was rubbing his eyes when suddenly the door to his lab was thrown open. He jerked his head around and saw a man standing there with a gun in his hand. He instinctively backed up a bit and raised his hands shoulder high. Only then did he speak.

"Hey, what do you want here?"

"Ah, Dr. Stockton, I presume?" Schroller said sarcastically.

"Don't shoot. Who are you and what do you want?"

"Someone who's going to help you with your research."

"How did you get in?"

"Shut up and listen," Schroller said sitting down on a stool while he kept the gun pointed at him. Stockton was about to say something, but Schroller waved the gun from him to the big screen and back to him.

"So, you are analyzing that, huh?"

"That's my job. Making a mathematical assessment of . . ." Stockton started explaining.

"Save me the details. I know it's a fake anyway."

"On the contrary, it's a real . . ."

Again, Schroller interrupted him.

"No, it isn't and that's what you will report."

"But I can't do that," Stockton protested.

Schroller got up and pointed the gun at Stockton's chest at close range.

"Oh yes, you can."

"You can't make me."

"Stand up and turn around," Schroller snapped.

A fearful Stockton turned around and for a moment considered taking a pen, a ruler, anything from his desk to use against this man, but feeling the gun between his shoulder blades caused him to reconsider.

Schroller fished a large plastic tie out of his pocket. He had already inserted one end into the locking slot and all he had to do was to slide Stockton's hands in it. He could do that with one hand. Once the plastic was around the wrists, he tugged on the end to tighten the loop. Stockton had almost no room to maneuver his hands and that's the way Schroller wanted it.

"So, we're finished here," he said, turning Stockton around and pushing him toward the door of the lab.

"Where are we going?" Stockton asked. "I need my phone."

"Good idea," Schroller laughed. "I almost forgot. You need make a call to relay your professional opinion about that painting."

"I'm not making any calls," Stockton protested.

"We'll see soon enough. Now, where is your phone?"

"In my jacket pocket."

"Great, let's get the jacket," Schroller said, grabbing it from a coat hanger. He then turned off the lights in the lab and pushed Stockton out. He made sure the door was locked. On their way down the stairs,

Stockton lost his balance a little but Schroller yanked him up by his tied wrists making Stockton scream with pain.

"Shut up! You don't want to me to have to shoot anyone do you?"

Stockton kept quiet and walked down the stairs. In the hallway, Schroller turned off the lights and opened the main door. He quickly checked for anyone walking by, but it was quiet except for a cab driving a block down the street. Schroller thrust Stockton quickly to the other side of the street. He opened the passenger door, shoved Stockton in, and closed the door. Schroller started the car and drove off.

"Now, just in case you try something," he said. "I can drive and shoot."

Stockton remained quiet, leaning forward, trying to relax his arms and hands.

It was past midnight when Schroller parked the Mercedes in front of the motel room. He had not said a word to Stockton during the whole drive, though the scientist had made several attempts to get a conversation going. Since the topic was invariably about what the meaning of all this was, and when he was going to let him go, Schroller had not bothered to reply and had turned on a rock station on the radio. Now that they were at the motel, Schroller yanked Stockton out of the car and unlocked the door to his room. He flung the door wide open. Isabelle woke up from a light sleep and immediately panicked, but a muffled scream was all she could muster. The tape over her mouth kept her from alarming any neighbors.

"Shut up, woman," he said while pushing Stockton inside. He closed the door and turned on the light.

"Got you some company."

He pushed Stockton down on the ground next to Isabelle's bed keeping his gun pointed at him.

"Let us go. What do you want with us anyway?" Stockton asked.

"Shut up," Schroller said and took the tape roll from the table, ripping a large piece off. He put it over Stockton's mouth.

"That's better. Tomorrow you'll find out why you're here. It will be a big day, so get some sleep."

He tied Stockton's ankles together, took a nylon strap and made Stockton sit at the foot of the bed with his hands toward a bed post. He then tied the strap to the plastic tie around his wrists and from there to the post, leaving little wriggle room. He made sure Stockton's phone was turned off completely, just as he had done with Isabelle's. He figured there was no need to have a nearby cell tower serve as a beacon to their whereabouts.

CHAPTER 27

Thursday Morning

TOM HAD GOTTEN up very early. Actually, he hadn't slept. Maybe he dozed off a few times, but the few hours in bed had been dominated by his mind going back and forth between Isabelle and the painting. He was worried about her and he had good reason to be. Schroller seemed desperate to get that painting and he was armed. The fact that he had been able to pull off the kidnapping in broad daylight and at the Metropolitan of all places, showed that he was cunning and prepared. What else would he do to get the painting? Not wanting to come up with an answer, Tom's thoughts drifted to the value of the painting and how that would make him a rich man, even though it might not be sold on Friday. He thought about that more and more, especially about the fact that the auction could be a vehicle to catch Schroller if the kidnapping, wasn't resolved. He imagined getting another painting that looked like *The Circumcision*, or having someone quickly paint a copy of it. He was sure Schroller wouldn't be able to tell the difference, but there was almost no time left. Then he thought the idea was stupid and turned onto his other side and started thinking about Isabelle again. He had tossed and turned the whole night long, jumping from one idea to another and this morning none of them made sense.

He checked his watch and decided that 6 a.m. was way too early to call Marco. His own hunt for Isabelle last night, driving from one motel to another, hadn't resulted in anything. If Marco had heard or discovered anything himself, he would have called him. Marco was committed to helping him and Tom was happy about that. On the other hand, it didn't make the situation between him and the ex-detective optimal.

He noticed that every time there was an opportunity, Marco would steer the conversation back to the way he ran his art store. That pissed him off every time. When was he going to get over the fact that he paid a high price for that historical document? I can set my own prices, Tom thought, so why not try to get the most out of a deal. After all, it was a family related document, and at the time Marco bought it, he really wanted it. Come to think of it, Tom recalled, I could have charged even more. And then there was this constant questioning about the pieces he was trying to sell now. Granted, he was lying in the case of the Qing vase, and selling stolen goods was illegal, but he needed cash in a hurry. If he was sure everything would work out with the Rembrandt, he could run a respectable store. Better yet, once everything was sold, he might even go into the curator business. He would love to be involved with very expensive paintings, and since he owned one . . .

He had made some strong coffee and was drinking his second cup as he focused on Isabelle again. If he could only talk to her, that would tell him something about how she was doing. She must know how horrible it would be to have to give up that painting. Maybe she would understand if he tried to slow down the arrangement to use it as ransom. He was sure Dr. Amado wouldn't be at his office yet. He wondered what he would say when he asked for the painting back. And where were the police in all this anyway? Were they any closer to finding Schroller? They had his car make and license plate and he must be driving in and out of the city. Surely they could get his tag number every time he went through a toll booth. Things like that always worked on TV shows, so why not now? If they only could find him and the place he was holding Isabelle, his own decision would be so much easier.

After another cup of coffee, he was tired of waiting and called Marco.

"Hey, heard anything from the police?"

"Good morning," Marco yawned, although he had been up for a while. "Nothing more than that they checked about twelve motels in the New Rochelle area and nothing turned up. He moved between cell towers and may not even be staying in that area. Just as he did with that motel room, he's throwing us off his track."

"Shit. I went to about ten motels last night. Nothing. I haven't heard from him either. What's he waiting for? He's got to arrange an exchange sooner or later."

"I agree. Now, about last night; have you sorted things out a bit?"

"Oh, yeah. I'm sorry. I was just upset last night. I swear I'm going to clean my act up. I'm off to the bank this morning and will talk to them. I'll try to pick up the painting before 10 a.m. You're right. I have no choice."

"Glad you see it that way. Keep your head up. It will all work out. They'll get him right after the drop. Call me or O'Grady as soon as he sets it up with you."

"They are looking for Isabelle, right?"

"Of course. We're tracking his cell phone and Isabelle's as well. Don't worry. We're on it."

"Okay. Talk to you later," Tom sighed, ready to hang up.

"Wait, one more thing," Marco said. "When he calls, tell him that a friend of yours is going to bring it. I'll do it myself. Make sure you insist on that."

"I'm not sure he'll go for that and why would you want to do that? You have no stake in this."

"Trust me. All he wants is that painting of yours and he'd rather see me than you make the drop. Actually then he wouldn't have to worry about me spying on him like last time."

"You're right. Okay, I'll try."

"It'll work out."

Everyone at Schroller's lair was awake early. Neither Isabelle nor Stockton had slept much, but Schroller seemed rested and ready to go. He opened the door a little bit and breathed in the fresh air. The stale air in the room had made him all stuffed up. He couldn't wait to get down to business this morning and collect the painting later. He quickly scanned the parking lot, but didn't see anything out of the ordinary. The sun had just come up and the huge motel sign lit up most of the cars. He closed the door, took his gun out and walked over to Stockton. He ripped the tape of his mouth and cut all straps.

"If you need to go, now is your chance," he said, pointing his gun toward the bathroom.

Stockton rubbed his wrists and ankles, slowly got up, and walked into the bathroom.

"Leave the door open," Schroller yelled and turned his attention to Isabelle who was making noises. He took the tape off and she gasped for air.

"Please, cut these straps. My arms are totally numb," she said with a distinctive hoarseness in her voice.

"Sure," Schroller said, cutting the strap around her wrists, leaving her ankles tied.

Isabelle was still rubbing her arms when Stockton came back from the bathroom. Schroller motioned with his gun to a chair near the small round table.

"Have a seat," he ordered. Stockton sat down and Schroller tied his wrists behind the chair. He then went over to Isabelle and cut the strap around her ankles.

"Your turn," he said.

It took a moment for Isabelle to find her balance as she walked to the bathroom. She slammed the door shut behind her and locked it, prompting Schroller to walk over to the door.

"Leave the door open!" he yelled.

"Give me some privacy, you moron. You open the door yourself!" she yelled back.

Schroller shrugged his shoulders and waited by the door.

Stockton leaned back enough so he wouldn't topple over. He parted the curtains a little with his head to see where they were. Schroller quickly pointed his gun at him.

"Hey! Leave that!"

"Why don't you let us go? We can't help you get that painting."

"Oh, you just wait and see," Schroller grinned and pounded on the door. "Hurry it up in there, time to come out!"

He heard the toilet flush and then Isabelle turned on the water. Inside, Isabelle was looking for some sort of weapon but couldn't find anything useful. She had expected an extra phone in the room, but this was a cheap motel. She considered staying in the locked bathroom, but she had seen Schroller's approach to locked doors and realized the futility of that. She dried her hands and put lotion on her wrists and ankles. They were red and chafed and the lotion stung. She opened the door, walked past Schroller without looking at him and sat down on the bed.

Schroller walked over to Stockton.

"Okay, Doc, ready for your fifteen minutes of fame?"

"We're hungry and we want something to drink."

"Later! It's time to make that call."

"What call?"

"To the museum, of course. What's the number of that curator at the museum?"

"You mean Dr. Amado?"

"Whatever his name is. The one who's waiting for your report."

"I don't remember his number."

"But you were going to call him this morning with the results, weren't you?"

"Yes, but the number is in the lab."

Stockton's stalling didn't bother Schroller too much. He'd dealt with situations like this before and knew exactly what to do. He turned to Isabelle.

"You, come over here and sit down," he said pointing with his gun from the bed to the other chair at the table.

"What can I do?" Isabelle asks, not getting up.

"Sit down here," Schroller demanded. "Now!"

Isabelle sat down and Schroller tied her wrists behind the chair. Her eyes widened with fear when he lit up a cigarillo, took a few drags and inspected the tip that was red hot.

"What are going to do?" she asked in a panic.

"Refreshing Dr. Stockton's memory here," Schroller laughed. He turned to Stockton.

Stockton also realized what their kidnapper was going to do and reacted.

"Leave her alone. She's got nothing to do with that painting."

"Oh, yes, she does. You see, Doctor, this young woman is the girlfriend of the man who owns the painting. So, she's got a lot to do with it. She even works at the museum."

"Don't you hurt her!" Stockton demanded.

"Well, do you remember the guy's number yet?"

"No, as I said, it's at the lab."

"I see," Schroller said, taking another drag from his cigarillo. He turned back to Isabelle and bent over so that his face was directly in front of hers.

"Of course, you know the number by heart, don't you?" he asked her.

"He's not in my department, I don't know it," she lied.

"Okay, let me refresh your memory, because I think you know the number," Schroller said, turning to Stockton.

He took his cigarillo and held it close to Stockton's cheek. Stockton felt the heat and leaned back. Schroller pulled Stockton's head closer to the cigarillo and held it there. Isabelle realized what was about to happen.

"NO!" she yelled, shaking her head.

"Ah, the little lady has something to say," Schroller said.

"Don't hurt him. I have the number," she blurted out.

Stockton threw her an angry look.

"Let's have it," Schroller demanded, ready to write it down.

Just before he dialed, Schroller stood in front of the table and looked at Stockton.

"Okay, here's how it's going to go. I'll dial the number and you do the talking. You tell this Amado that your conclusion is solid and without doubt. The painting is not by Rembrandt but a very good forgery with original materials and so on. If he asks for details, make sure that you throw some of your mathematical stuff at him. Make it convincing and final, but keep it short."

"What's that going to get you?"

"A cheap painting that's easy to part with."

"What if I refuse?"

"Slow learner, huh?" Schroller asked while he pushed up the left sleeve of Isabelle's blouse. Schroller pulled Isabelle's arm toward him, took a few drags from his cigarillo and blew on the tip. He held it an inch away from Isabelle's bare arm. She pulled her arm back as far away as she could, but Schroller's grasp was firm.

"I'm sure the lady can handle this."

"Okay, okay. Make the call."

Schroller released his grip on Isabelle's arm and dialed the number. He held the phone to Stockton's ear. With his right hand he held the cigarillo up and kept it hot.

The call connected.

"Dr. Amado?" Stockton asked.

"Dr. Stockton. What's the good news?"

"I'm afraid it's not. After thorough analysis, I've concluded that the painting is a forgery. A good one, but a forgery nonetheless."

It was quiet for a moment. It was Dr. Amado who broke the awkward silence.

"I'm stunned. It's almost unbelievable. We saw it as real and Mr. van Weteren is sure."

"Well, it's a fine piece of forgery. The probability of it being a Rembrandt is way below the threshold."

Schroller leaned over towards Stockton's other ear.

"Wrap it up now," he whispered.

"Well, I'm disappointed to say the least. Can we meet?"

"I'm sorry, not now. Bye," Stockton said as Schroller took the phone from him.

With the cigarillo in his mouth Schroller sat on one of the beds, took a deep drag and blew the smoke in the air.

"Now, that was nice work. You'll be out of here in no time."

CHAPTER 28

Thursday Mid-morning

THE RESTORATION ROOM at the Metropolitan was the least likely meeting place in the museum. People wore white jackets and donned gloves and hats. Not that the room was entirely sterile, but it was clean and clutter free. This morning there were no restorers or technicians in the room. There were four people and one painting on a slanted table and it was the subject of the discussion at hand. Dr. Amado and Mr. van Weteren were sitting at a table with the museum director and Jonathan Metzer of Sotheby's. After the call from Stockton, Dr. Amado had gone to the room where van Weteren was studying the burned part of the painting and had called the others, inviting them to join them as soon as possible. Jonathan was the last to arrive and after closing the door, Dr. Amado told them about Dr. Stockton's findings.

"Stockton was sure. His track record is great and we've relied on his mathematical techniques."

"I am really puzzled," van Weteren said, rubbing his chin, staring at nothing in particular on the table. I haven't missed a Rembrandt in thirty years. I'm at a loss for words."

"I'm really sorry about this. I guess that changes the auction arrangement?" Metzer asked, looking at the director and Dr. Amado.

"I'm afraid it does. Are you aware of the disappointment this will be for our museum?" Dr. Amado asked.

"Yes, of course. I'm well aware of the arrangements with Mr. Arden. I'll talk to him about the auction when I get back to the office," Metzer said.

"I would wait with that. I'm not totally accepting the assessment," Dr. Amado said.

Van Weteren stood up and was standing still in front of the canvas. "Do you think Stockton made a mistake then?"

"To be honest," Dr. Amado said, pushing his chair back from the table so he could face van Weteren, "Something bothers me about the way he said it. He's usually much more verbose and he never starts to go into detail on the phone. He usually comes here and we go over everything."

"So, what are you going to do?" van Weteren asked.

"Well, for now, I'm not going to announce Stockton's findings. I hope he stops by later today so I can go over his results with him."

"Good idea. Tell him that we're not changing our minds. Everyone at the Rembrandt Research Project is sure this is a genuine Rembrandt and we consider it extremely fortunate that someone saved this painting from what was obviously a big fire a long time ago."

"This is indeed the first time that there has been such a big discrepancy in the authentication findings, those of our own curators and those of Dr. Stockton," the director said. "I agree we should wait for him to explain the results in person."

"I have a flight at 6 p.m. because I'm needed back in Amsterdam tomorrow. I need to leave here at 3 p.m. at the latest."

"I understand," Dr. Amado said. "We have your notes and remarks. We'll send you an email with his report. You'll probably have it by the time you get to your desk tomorrow morning."

"All right, I'm leaving now. I'll be in the office all day. Call me before the end of the day," Metzer said, getting up. "Since Mr. Arden isn't aware of any this, I'll wait to hear from you before I call him."

"I'll talk to you later then. Have a good day," Dr. Amado said, shaking hands with Metzer.

The director showed Metzer out. Dr. Amado joined van Weteren in front of the painting.

"You see here?" van Weteren asked, pointing at the edge of the burn on the canvas.

Dr. Amado leaned in close and looked through the magnifying glass. Van Weteren explained.

"As you know, painters in Rembrandt's time used a layered method of applying paint. First he put a white lead-primed support on the canvas, then a thin brownish monochrome. Look closely at that edge where the heat of the fire exposed the cascade of layers."

"I see it, yes."

"The next layer is really thick, especially where the light is most intense. He then tooled and shaped the paint to create a clever impasto characteristic, thereby allowing him to let light reflect the way he wanted. He was a master at this. I just wanted to point out that here we see this process in front of us."

Dr. Amado stepped away from the painting.

"Truly a Rembrandt," he said.

By the time Tom got to the store, he was totally confused. Not having had enough rest during the night clouded his judgment. The promise he made less than an hour ago to Marco was the driving force of his intention. If only he could buy more time, not only for the police to find her, but especially for Schroller to see his reaction if turning over the ransom was delayed. It was thinking like this that had made him totally indecisive again, and when he sat down at his desk, he didn't know what to do. He knew he should have called Dr. Amado already in order to have the painting packaged up, but he just didn't have the courage. Twenty to thirty million dollars on the line, and what if the cops couldn't track Schroller down right away? Would they get another chance at the airport? He had to get it back to Germany somehow. Did he make other arrangements so that he didn't have to carry the painting? Tom had no idea, and tapped his fingers on his desk. Visions of Isabelle shot through his mind. How was she doing? How was she holding up? He needed to hear her voice. As long as Schroller was going to text him, he wouldn't have a chance to talk to her if she was with him. He figured Schroller wasn't using his phone to communicate from where he was holding Isabelle. That call through a cell tower in New Rochelle was indeed meant to throw them all off, just like Marco had said. For all he knew, she was being held downtown in one of the fancy hotels. Schroller hadn't been seen around any motels he had visited, so where was he? Where was Isabelle?

It took Tom another fifteen minutes to make up his mind. He decided to text Schroller. If he read the message while he was with Isabelle, the cops might get his location. He carefully typed in the text:

"Cannot possibly get the painting today. Problems at the Met. Maybe tomorrow."

He closed his phone after he heard the tone confirming that his message was sent. Now he had to wait.

CHAPTER 29

Thursday Noon

TOM'S MESSAGE WAS not well received. Schroller had driven to a beach area on Long Island, just in case someone was tracking his cell phone. Using simple triangulation, they would figure out his whereabouts in a hurry and with all that was at stake, this was not a mistake he could make. As long as he was on the move he didn't mind being traced, he'd just be careful. Consequently, after reading Tom's lousy excuse, he turned off his phone immediately. He threw it on the passenger seat and took off right away to the motel.

Before he had left the room, Isabelle had insisted on getting food. He was hungry too, and on the way back he had stopped at McDonalds. When he arrived back at the motel Isabelle and Stockton devoured their food. He cleaned up, tied Stockton back to the bed, while Isabelle sat at the table. He put tape over their mouths.

While sipping his coffee, he considered his next move. He had assumed it wouldn't get that far, but given the resistance by Tom, there was no other way. During some past extortion and kidnapping stints it had usually been the police that used delaying tactics and peripheral mind-playing games. He had never met such a stubborn man as Tom. He could hardly believe that he wouldn't do anything to get his girlfriend back. In this case the ransom was even easier to get. There was no large amount of money involved, so the time to get that together was not an issue here. So why not get the painting and get it over with? Most people would, once they knew it was a forgery, but Tom's decision was an incredible mistake. He needed to be taught a lesson and one he would never forget. Schroller had said as much to Isabelle when he had come back to the room. She'd asked what he meant and he had told her she'd find out after she had eaten.

Schroller got up and lit a cigarillo. He put it in the ashtray and took the roll of tape.

"Give me your right hand," he demanded.

Isabelle pulled her arm back instantly, but he grabbed it and slammed her wrist on the arm of the chair. He held her hand down tight while he taped it to the chair.

"Now your left hand," he said.

Again, Isabelle resisted, but Schroller was too strong for her and he forced her hand on the other arm of the chair. Likewise he taped her left hand. He took a large strip of the tape and put it across her chest and as he unrolled more tape, looped it to the back of the chair and back in front of her. He did this twice until he felt sure it was tight and she had no room to move. He took the hotel phone from the night stand and brought it to the table. He dragged the other chair in front of her and sat down, picking up the cigarillo. He took a few drags and knocked off the ashes, revealing the red tip.

"Now, your turn," he said as he sat down, picking up the cigarillo.

"What are you going to do?" Isabelle asked, trying to hide the fear in her voice.

"A special treat for your boyfriend," Schroller said dryly.

"Why? Isn't he going to give you that painting?" Isabelle asked.

"Well, he's not ready to pay the ransom, so he needs something to hurry him up."

"And the painting is the ransom, right?"

"Of course, but apparently he has some issues getting it from the museum."

Isabelle didn't answer right away. Surely, if Tom wanted the painting, Dr. Amado would oblige. But she knew Tom, and although normally he would have a hard time parting with a valuable painting, it shouldn't be an issue after Dr. Stockton's call this morning. Surely, Tom must know that the painting was worthless by now, so why the hold up, she wondered.

"Well, maybe he doesn't know about it being a so-called forgery, or the museum is having some issues. There is an exhibition and . . ." she started, but Schroller interrupted her.

"No need to excuse him. It's his responsibility and he fell short, again. So this time he'll regret it," he said, taking the motel phone off the hook. He dialed.

"Arden Arts," Tom answered.

Schroller started singing a children's tune much like the end of *Pop! Goes the Weasel*, but he put different words to the song.

"Time to pay the ransom," he taunted.

"Listen, I can't get the painting from the Met."

"It's worthless to you now."

"Why don't you let Isabelle go? She's got nothing to do with this."

Schroller laughed loudly.

"On the contrary! She wants to talk to you about this," he said, holding the phone to Isabelle's ear.

"Tom? Tom is that you?" she asked excitedly, but Schroller abruptly took the phone away.

"See?" he asked speaking into the phone, cutting Tom off as he was about to answer Isabelle. "I've got her, she loves you, and you have the painting. If you want her back, surely, the painting is a small sacrifice. I guess you still think you can get lots of money for it."

"Damn straight!

"Suit yourself. Go ahead and call the Met and you'll see that they'll be happy to give it back to you."

"I don't think so."

"Well, your girlfriend here is going to be really pissed at you for holding out."

"What are you talking about?"

"Let me give you a little preview of how persuasive I can be."

Schroller put the phone down on the table with the speaker facing Isabelle. Tom heard some noise but couldn't figure out what was going on.

"What are you doing?"

Schroller taped Isabelle's mouth again. No need to alarm other people at the motel he thought. He took a few more drags on his cigarillo, took it out of his mouth and blew the tip clean so that it was glowing red. If he had heard Tom, he didn't show it. Quite unexpectedly to Isabelle, he touched the glowing ashes to her upper arm. It happened so fast that she couldn't pull away. Within a split second she felt the searing pain and she screamed. It was barely audible as her screams were muffled by the tape. She pulled her arm back as far as she could, tears running freely down her cheek. Schroller held the phone up closer to Isabelle who was screaming even louder, as the shooting pain of cauterized and severed nerve endings engulfed her whole being.

Tom kept yelling at Schroller, asking him what was going on. He had heard enough to recognize the noise as a distant scream. He knew he was hurting Isabelle, and he asked him to stop. There was no answer from Schroller.

Schroller touched her arm again with the tip of the cigarillo and Isabelle screamed in even greater agony.

"So, that should do it for now," he said and put the cigarillo in the ash tray. He picked up the phone and pulled one corner of the tape off her mouth. All Tom heard was a short scream. Schroller put the tape back and spoke into the phone.

"You see what you have caused?" he asked, staring at the red burned spots on Isabelle's arm, not even blinking an eye. "I can do this all day. You know what, I'll call you tomorrow. I'm having too much fun today. This time, be ready to bring me the painting or you will not see her alive again."

He slammed the phone down without waiting for a reply.

"So, *Fraulein*," he said getting up. "That'll hurt for a while, but it will get better by the time I'm back."

He left Isabelle where she was. He made sure his phone was in airplane mode with the GPS on, and then took a close-up picture of her arm.

Tom sat at his office desk in shock and stared at his phone for a few moments after Schroller hung up on him. He closed his eyes and rubbed his forehead.

"Dammit. This guy is nuts. What's he doing to her? Why can't they find this fucking bastard?" he asked out loud.

He jumped up taking his phone and dialed.

"Marco, where are you?" he asked, almost begging.

"I'm still at the police station. What's going on? Let me put you on speaker phone so O'Grady can listen in."

"He's torturing Isabelle! I don't know exactly what he did but I heard screams as if he was hurting her!"

O'Grady nodded his head but didn't say anything.

"I need you to stay calm Tom. I know this is distressing, but we're dealing with an international criminal here. What did he ask you?"

"For the painting of course."

"You didn't say that you needed more time did you?"

"Well, I just can't walk into the Met and get the painting can I?

"I can't believe you. I thought we had settled that. Have you even called them?

"I'll call now." Tom said, feeling more guilt.

"Did you get Schroller's number?"

"It came up as private number. It was not his usual number. Is anyone tracing these calls to me?"

"They're doing their best, Tom. Now, call the Met and get the damn painting. If he calls, set up the exchange right away and don't forget to tell him that someone else will have the painting."

"He's already changed the schedule and wants it tomorrow. I have a meeting with the bank and I'll arrange to pick up the painting then."

"If he has told you tomorrow, you won't hear from him again today. That gives us a little more time to find him. Sit tight and I'll stop by the store this afternoon."

Tom hung up and dialed Dr. Amado's direct number. There was no answer and he left a short voice message to call him as soon as possible. He then dialed the Met's number and got an operator who asked who was calling for Dr. Amado.

"Tell him Tom Arden is calling, and it's urgent."

He waited for a while and the woman told him that Dr. Amado wasn't available at this time, 'Could she take a message'?

"No, thank you," he said and hung up.

Dr. Amado had seen the first call from Tom but had decided to let it ring. No need to get him all upset, he figured. As soon as Dr. Stockton could come in and explain things, there would be plenty of time to discuss the situation.

When the second call came in, he told the operator that he was busy and asked if she would take a message.

At the precinct the team assigned to the kidnapping case was working non-stop, following leads on Schroller and his car. They were looking for him with a photo they had received from Interpol, a far better picture than the one from the DVR at the Met. On a wall visible to all in the incident room, there were several large display screens, roughly two feet wide and four feet in length. The one on the left showed a map of the greater New York City area. Every time Schroller's cell phone was used, a pin prick showed up automatically and a loud ping sounded. The longer he stayed on the phone, the stronger the ping was and a team could be dispatched at a moment's notice to that location. When he moved, new pin pricks showed up, allowing them to trace the movement of the phone. There were hits on the map in Manhattan, one in Brooklyn, several in New Rochelle and one on Long Island. Every pin prick had a time stamp below it so Schroller's could be traced along a time line. The screen in the center showed Isabelle's picture with the date and time she was kidnapped. Underneath the DVR pictures from the Met's security system were playing continuously. The screen on the right contained keywords and other information relevant to the case. The words RANSOM=PAINTING, BLACK MERCEDES, and the license plate number of Schroller's car were shown in a big font.

The screen to the right was updated with the words EXCHANGE FRIDAY.

O'Grady was at his desk with Marco. He leaned back in his chair.

"Don't know Marco. Something's not right here. Why does he want to risk another exchange?"

"I don't think it's going to be an exchange. He'll want to make sure it's the painting first, and then he might release her."

"After he arranges the drop, he'll have to be on the phone constantly to tell you where to go. We can trace him quickly even if he uses a new phone. As long as he's talking to you, we will know which cell makes contact with you and he'll pop up on the screen. We should be able to locate him quickly before he takes off with the painting."

"I agree, but I see a problem. I don't think Tom wants to part with it. Just taking it out of the Met will be a challenge, because I think Schroller might try to steal it right away there."

"That part I'll have covered. He'll be protected from the moment he steps out of that building. My men will be outside and follow him until he gives the painting to you and then you'll be on our radar. Hopefully we'll get him in time."

"Let's hope so. I'm not too keen on this whole thing, but I promised Tom I'd help him out. He's a loose cannon and we just can't let him do this drop."

"It sounds like Schroller really put the fear into him. We know from Interpol that Schroller is notorious for kidnapping and extortion. He puts pressure on by torturing his victims if things don't go his way. He's wanted in Germany on all sorts of charges. It's a surprise to us that he's operating in the US."

"That's exactly why I should do the drop. Tom's emotional state may screw this up and he may inadvertently push Schroller to escalate all this."

"Don't worry. We'll be there when you take the painting from Tom and we'll make sure there's a tracking device with the painting."

Marco finished his coffee and was about to leave for Tom's office, when his phone rang. It was Tom calling again.

"Marco. Listen, I just got a call from someone at NYU. Apparently, Dr. Stockton is missing. They found my number and called me to see if I knew where he was. I have no clue, but I know that he was working on the authentication of the painting."

Marco sat back down and frowned.

"Really? There may be a connection here."

"Yeah, that's my guess. Can you check into this?"

"Okay, we're on it. Also let me know when you hear from Schroller.

Marco closed his phone and sat back while O'Grady was waiting for him to say something. Marco snapped his fingers and stood up.

"There's this NYU professor, a Dr. Stockton, who was working with the painting and he's gone missing."

"So what are you thinking?"

"There's a good chance Schroller has something to do with it."

"Probably, but we need to make sure."

"You guys check with his family. I'm going to check something else," Marco said, grabbing his jacket. "I'll keep you posted."

About fifteen minutes later, Marco got to the NYU building on 78th Street. He wasn't sure where Stockton's office was, but judging from the list of departments, he guessed Curatorial Studies was the best guess. He ran up the stairs to the second floor and stopped by the first office on his right. The departmental secretary was actually the one who had made the call to Tom.

"Yes, we found the man's number on Dr. Stockton's desk. His assistant gave it to me. He's in the third room on the right."

"Thank you," Marco said and left.

The door sign simply read *Lab* and Marco opened the door. A young man was standing by a desk reading a notebook, and looked up when Marco entered.

"May I help you?" he asked.

"Yes. We got a call about Dr. Stockton not showing up for work this morning."

"Right. I thought it was strange because no matter how long he works at night, he's always in by nine. But that's not the only thing. He left the analysis running and his email was opened."

Marco was staring at the big screen.

"That's a copy of the Rembrandt"

"How do you know that?"

"I'm familiar with the case. By the way, my name is Marco Vincente," Marco said offering his hand.

"I'm Barry Edelstein. What do mean by *case?*" Barry asked, shaking Marco's hand.

"The owner of the painting needed some protection and this is an expensive painting."

"You're right about that. I was just looking over Dr. Stockton's notebook and from everything I see, the scans were all analyzed and the entropy of the overlaying masks in a state transition format is consistent with Rembrandt's . . ."

"So, it's real," Marco interrupted him.

"From what I can tell, yes," Barry said. "I'm not fully trained, but these high numbers are a slam dunk."

Marco looked even closer at a screen with a detail of the painting.

"So, just looking at this image you couldn't tell whether this is a real Rembrandt, but some mathematical calculation and poof . . . , when the smoke clears, you know it is? Amazing," Marco said, shaking his head.

"Well, there was a lot of research that went into this and Dr. Stockton is an expert in Rubens and Rembrandt."

"I see. Now, where do you think he could be?"

"No idea. I called his house number and his cell phone several times. All I can tell is that he left in a hurry last night. As I told you, he left everything running and his car keys are still here."

"Why didn't you tell me that right away?" Marco asked, reaching for his phone. He dialed O'Grady.

"Now, you're sure he's not in the building?" he asked Barry who shook his head as O'Grady answered.

"Marco here. Listen, I'm over at NYU at Dr. Stockton's lab. My first guess is that he's been kidnapped."

"I'll send over a team. Stay there."

"I'm sure it's Schroller."

CHAPTER 30

Thursday Noon

TOM WAS GOING crazy sitting in his office. The police weren't any help as far as he could tell and Marco wasn't getting anywhere either. He realized that his text message had probably triggered something really bad for Isabelle and not only did he feel guilty about that, he also felt very sad and helpless. Isabelle was in pain. He wanted to tell her how sorry he was. He had tried her cell phone several times, hoping that it would be on. Marco had told him that they were tracing all cell phones but that method had proven useless since her phone was most likely turned off. There was no way he could let Isabelle stay in the hands of that bastard much longer. He had to be drawn out. So why not send him another message saying that he had the painting at his store and he could come and get it?

He composed a short message to that effect, not really expecting an answer. But what if there was an answer? He clicked *Send*. He figured he'd better let the cops know. They should be here, staking out the place if Schroller showed up. Yes, that was brilliant, but just as he started to call, his phone rang. It was Marco.

"Hey, were your ears ringing?" Tom asked.

"How's that?"

"I was just about to call you."

"Your timing is perfect."

"Any good news?"

"I'm afraid not. Not only can't we find Schroller and Isabelle, but we're pretty sure that he's also kidnapped that Dr. Stockton."

"Are you kidding me?" Tom asked. "Do you have that confirmed?"

"No, there's been no demand for ransom or anything, but every sign points to his abduction."

"So, he's got two hostages now?"

"That's my guess."

"But what would he want with Dr. Stockton? All he was doing was a scientific analysis of the painting. More like a confirmation really because the Rembrandt Research Project people had declared it to be genuine."

"I hear you. Dr. Stockton's assistant also said as much from looking over Dr. Stockton's notes. I didn't quite understand what they really did, but the outcome was positive."

"That's good news, of course, but it doesn't help Isabelle."

"I agree Tom. Like you said, he'll be calling you tomorrow and most likely we'll be able to track him down. He'll lead us to Isabelle and Stockton and that should be the end of it."

"And I'll be out an authentic Rembrandt."

"Forget about the painting, Tom. We'll leave it up to the police to recover that. With a little luck, you'll have it back before the auction."

"Well, that's why I decided to try to speed things up a little."

"What do you mean? What have you done now?"

"I sent another text message, telling him the painting will be at my store this afternoon."

"I know you want to help Tom, but you really don't think Schroller is just going to drive over and collect the painting do you?"

"You never know."

"You invited an armed man into your store? Not that he's going to walk into a trap like that. Besides, you don't even have the painting."

"The cops could stake out my place."

"I think it's a waste of resources, but they'll send out some people. If I were you, I'd leave the store. Go home or go and visit some of your clients."

"I can do that."

"O'Grady's team is handling tons of leads and it takes a lot of time to track them all down. I think every black Mercedes in the city and the boroughs has been reported and checked out."

"Good. Have they gotten any more reports from motels or hotels?"

"A few dead leads. His picture is all over the place. I even saw a blurb on TV yesterday. Believe me, the entire task force is busy."

"All right. I guess I'll leave now. Call me the moment you hear anything."

"Will do. The cops should be around your area in no time. And, one more thing, let Schroller contact you, not the other way around."

"Okay, I promise," Tom said and ended the call.

He took a few of his index cards, locked up the store and walked over to the diner up the street. He would make his calls from there. If Schroller showed up, the cops would handle him. If he didn't show within a couple of hours, they'd probably call off the stake out.

At the diner he sat down with a cup of coffee but didn't make any calls. He couldn't stop thinking about Isabelle. He doubted Schroller would be caught before tomorrow morning.

CHAPTER 31

Thursday Afternoon

S CHROLLER LEFT THE motel room again because he needed to scout the drop area. He drove to the nearest station for the L Train on Dekalb Avenue in Brooklyn and parked his car two blocks away, under a large tree. He left the keys inside and didn't lock it. He took the train into the city and switching lines often, trying to stay out of the proximity of cameras. This wasn't easy but he wasn't terribly worried. He'd seen an old picture of himself on TV last night, since the kidnapping of Isabelle was pretty much in the forefront on the local news channels. A black wig and mustache had changed his appearance. Looking in the mirror in his car earlier, he had laughed out loud because now he looked more like a gangster than the blond handsome German he was portrayed to be. He hadn't bothered to change his clothes, so he still wore jeans and a black leather jacket.

Once he had walked out onto the streets of New York, he went inside a drug store but not to buy anything. He looked for a vantage point from which he would be able to see someone with a large package. He found one near the window. From there he could see people leaving the subway and that was essential. He then walked to a small bookstore and talked to the manager for a short while.

After leaving the store, he walked quickly back to the station and got on a train. Three stops later he got off, crossed the platform and got onto a train of another line. He did that two more times until he was satisfied. Leaving the station, he briefly turned on his phone and saw that he had one message.

He read Tom's latest message, shook his head and turned his phone off. He hailed a cab.

"If he thinks I will walk into a trap, he's crazy," he thought and got in. Anyone looking for him would have seen his phone signal in New York, but by the time they could get someone there, he'd be long gone.

Twenty minutes later he walked through Central Park toward the Metropolitan Museum. It amazed him that there were so many people walking, riding and sitting on benches all the time. He wondered whether any of them ever worked since it was the middle of the afternoon on a Thursday. People of all ages were using the park, doing all sorts of things. Although he couldn't care less, he still wondered. The picture he had formed of Americans being lazy was confirmed again he thought. As he neared the museum he became more careful because he saw a couple of policemen standing near their car on the corner of the building. A quick inspection told him that the other corner was likewise covered. He took a long detour to the front of the building and saw the same situation there. At the entrance there were four uniformed men who seemed to be casually hanging around, but they were actually looking at everyone on the steps, the sidewalk and those entering the building. He approached the loading dock area on the side. There were no policemen, but they could easily spot someone from one of the corners. On the other hand, when a truck would be parked there like now, their vision would be obstructed. The small truck was parked near the dock and there were a few men running around. According to the advertisement on the sides of the truck, it belonged to an interior decorating firm in the city and the big door behind the truck was wide open. The men were wearing jeans and black sweatshirts with the white company logo on it. The truck and the sweatshirts advertised the company as DECO DECORATE.

Checking his map, Schroller changed direction and walked toward New York Avenue. From a distance he recognized the Sotheby's building. He was relieved to see that there were no police cars or cops around. He walked up to the entrance, briefly checked out the lobby area through the glass windows and then crossed the street. He observed the building from the other side and soon crossed the street again. This time he walked up the steps and went inside.

"Just in case," he said to himself.

Two hours later, he arrived at a house in Brooklyn. He had used public transportation only. The house was rather small but had a large warehouse at the back that you could only access from another street behind the house. Next to the house was a large sign that indicated that the business was an International Shipping Agency specializing in secure transports to Europe and the Middle East. He rang the doorbell twice and waited. After a short while, a man opened the door halfway.

"Schroller?" the man asked.

Schroller nodded and stepped inside when the man opened the door all the way. He followed him into a small office that had once been a living room. The man behind the desk got up and spoke in German to Schroller.

"Do you have the package ready to ship?"

"No, not yet. I'll have it at the latest tomorrow, late afternoon," Schroller said, sitting down and lighting up a cigarillo.

"I hope so! We need to send the container on Monday and we'll have a little work left to do," the man said.

"I'll bring it in time, don't worry," Schroller said and then paused. "I do have a favor to ask though."

"Tell me, your account is good with us."

"I need a car for a day."

"You can use mine," the man said. "Where's your rental?"

"Parked near a subway station here in Brooklyn," Schroller said, showing the location on a map that was lying on the desk.

"We'll call it in once you're in the air," the man said.

"Perfect," Schroller smiled. "Now, I need a few more things. Get me a delivery truck by ten tomorrow morning at your garage in Manhattan. I'll be bringing it back there within an hour and I will need a limo then. Make it a big one. I need one of your drivers to stay with me all the way to JFK. Can you arrange that? I have a Lufthansa flight at 6:30 p.m."

"I can do that. Leave my Toyota at the garage."

"Perfect. When the limo driver goes back to the garage, he can drive the package over here and you take it from there."

"You're good," the man smiled and shook hands with Schroller.

Schroller drove the beige Toyota by Tom's office. It took him two tries to finally spot some action. Two police cars were parked on side streets and he assumed there were several unmarked cars around. Two men were unloading meaningless stuff into the office next to Tom's. Obviously undercover cops, he smiled. One man was tinkering with a car and another was window shopping. Schroller had seen enough and left the area. His suspicion of the police being involved was confirmed and he was glad he had changed his look. Switching cars had been necessary as well because the latest news mentioned that the police were looking for a black Mercedes. Finding it now would not help them any more. As for tomorrow's plans, he felt good about them. Everything was covered and unless he walked into a cop's arms, there was no way they would catch him. By this time tomorrow he would be ready to board a plane, and the painting would be set on its own route. Another job well done.

Tom had been tracking down the customer who was interested in the statue. He hadn't shown up as he said he would. From the diner he had made several calls, but had no luck. He left messages for several people, including the one for the Qing vase, but it seemed like everyone was out and about on this beautiful sunny afternoon. He had called Marco about an hour ago, but there was no news. Apparently O'Grady and his team were banking on the drop tomorrow when Schroller would have to show himself. It had been over 24 hours now since the kidnapping of Isabelle. The newspaper had mentioned that a ransom was demanded but it was not clear how much money was involved. When Tom read that, he shook his head.

As he drank his third cup of coffee, he reflected on how he would do things differently next time. Immediately he dismissed the thought. There would never be a second chance for something like this to happen again. He realized that his first mistake had been to text Kevin about the painting. The Met would have kept it quiet if he had asked. He also should have arranged a one-on-one sale, but it was too late now. The auction had to happen. If anything went wrong tomorrow and the painting was not handed over, then Schroller had only one chance left and that was to come to the auction. Of course with the cops all over, it didn't matter what Schroller did, as long as he didn't hurt Isabelle any more. Surely, tomorrow's drop would bring out every cop in New

York. He hoped that they would consider what was at stake. There was the painting on the one hand, and the two kidnapping victims on the other hand. He was sure that nobody would want to jeopardize the well being of Isabelle or Stockton. What if Schroller got the painting and didn't reveal where they were being held? What if, and he could hardly bring himself to think this, he had killed them? Enough of all this, the thought. He called over the waitress.

Tom paid his bill when Marco called.

"Any news?"

"Nothing yet. We figure that the drop will be in the city, not only because they just got a signal from his phone there, but because he'll think that he can get away easier. We learned that he likes to work in big cities, and he's very smart. He'll be hard to catch, but as you know I'll be closer to him than anyone."

"With the tracer in the package you should be able to find him quickly, right?"

"It will be dicey. The first thing he's going to do is check for that. No, that trace is only valid for a short while, but it should be active long enough for the police to see him."

"So, how is O'Grady going to go about it?"

"By the time Schroller gets his hands on the package, they'll be within fifty yards and establish that visual contact. They won't pick him up but will follow him. If he goes to an airport or something, they'll stop him. If he goes to another location, like a motel, or a place where he could be holding the hostages, they'll let him lead them there and then get him. So, one way or another, you can count on getting the painting back."

"Wait a minute, what happens if Isabelle and Stockton aren't found? How are they going to force him to tell them where they are?"

"They have their ways."

"I'm not so sure and I think it's a flaw. What if he demands to be able to leave the country before he'll reveal the whereabouts of the Isabelle?"

"They won't let it get that far."

"How?"

"They'll quickly promise him a deal if he cooperates."

"I think O'Grady and his team are watching too much TV."

"C'mon Tom, they've been through things like this before. Don't worry. We'll keep you in the loop."

"That's fine, but I just want to run another scenario by you."

"You're not thinking of stalling again are you?"

"Wait, hear me out. Everybody knows that Schroller is desperate to get that painting. He's already kidnapped two people, possibly tortured them and we don't know what else he's capable of. But the one thing that occupies his mind is that painting. What if he realizes that this painting can only be gotten at the auction tomorrow afternoon? He'd know it would be a trap, but he would do anything to get it. He's basically blinded by the idea of getting his hands on it. So, what if we let him? The police can still use their tactics of negotiating with him. What do you think?"

"Tom, we've been through this before. What if he kills the hostages before he executes this last attempt? We can't run that risk. You've already taunted him and you heard the result. Unless something changes with respect to Isabelle and Stockton, I'd say we need to stick to the plan."

"Well, at least do me a favor and run it by O'Grady, will you?"

"There's no point to it, Tom."

"Just do it, please. I'd like to know what he thinks."

CHAPTER 32

Thursday Evening

S CHROLLER RETURNED TO the motel room feeling pretty good. He had successfully scouted all venues for possible scenarios. Of course, he preferred his first choice since that gave him the best opportunity to pull this whole thing off. There was one item he still had to take care of, but Isabelle would have to help him with that. If everything went according to plan, the drop would be in the city at a place of his choosing. Isabelle would be close enough so that in case something went wrong, she'd be right there to use as his insurance. If it all worked out, she'd be in the same position that he planned to leave Dr. Stockton in, and that was simply that she would be missing. Maybe those smart cops would find one of them, or both, or neither one. Ah, he mused, such are the consequences of playing games with the German mind.

Upon entering the room he threw a late evening paper on the table and dropped more McDonald's food on the bed. He ripped the tapes off his victims' mouths and untied their wrists. They each drank a small bottle of water with urgency. Isabelle didn't eat the cheeseburger right away. She was in pain and she felt exhausted because of lack of sleep during the thirty hours or so that Schroller had kept her here.

"When are you going to let us go?" she asked while Stockton looked up, having just stuffed his mouth with French fries.

"Your time will come. Your boyfriend wanted to exchange you for the painting this afternoon already, but he did not stick to the rules."

"What do you mean?"

"His place was surrounded by cops, even though I said not to involve the police."

"Did you talk to Tom?"

"Never even saw him."

Stockton stopped eating for a second and looked at Schroller.

"How was the news received about the painting being a forgery?" he asked.

"Funny you should ask that. I checked the paper and found nothing about that. Apparently, the museum has neglected to tell the press about your incredible findings." Schroller said and then turned to Isabelle again.

"You know, I'm not even sure that your boyfriend knows about it yet. Now, why would that curator keep this important information from the media and your boyfriend, huh?"

Isabelle had been thinking about that and had an answer she didn't like, but at the same time she realized that Schroller should know that, in all likelihood, Dr. Amado had played it cool without panicking.

"I think he didn't believe Dr. Stockton. Plain and simple. He's waiting for a personal meeting with him and until he's very sure, only then, will he inform Tom."

"Maybe we need to give that Dr. Amado another call," Schroller offered.

"It wouldn't do any good. You underestimated how the authentication process works. It's not just about one negative opinion. It's a collection of tests and opinions. Dr. Stockton's just offered one of them and if his is the only one that is negative, a little more explanation would be needed."

"Well, he can't wait forever, and I know for a fact that Dr. Stockton's results are as important as the one of the best expert the Met has brought in."

Isabelle didn't reply as she figured it was no good arguing with Schroller. She took a bite of her cheeseburger. She never ate fast food and although she was hungry, she didn't enjoy eating cold food that was supposed to be eaten warm.

Dr. Stockton finished eating his fries and burgers and decided to chime in on the suggestion to make another call. Maybe he could get away with something.

"I'll make another call to Dr. Amado and explain my results," he offered.

"No, I think he got the message. Tom is going to find out soon that he has a forgery and I'll have that painting soon." Schroller said, reconsidering his previous idea.

He had enough of the conversation and tied Isabelle's wrists again. He did the same to Stockton and put tape over their mouth. Satisfied that they couldn't make noise or escape, he sat down and turned the TV on for the evening news. Isabelle's kidnapping was still the main news, but no mention was made of the kidnapping of Dr. Stockton. He thought that this was actually good. If they knew he was kidnapped, they might conclude that his assessment of the painting was coerced. As long as he was just missing, there was no problem. Consequently there also wasn't anything said about the nature of the painting, being real or not. It wasn't until a reporter asked the police commissioner what the ransom demand was for the release of Isabelle, that the public found out that it was an old, valuable painting. He could not comment any further and the reported didn't press on. Schroller turned the TV off.

CHAPTER 33

Friday Morning

THE CHAIR IN the bank's office was uncomfortable. The back was flat and straight up. Tom tried to find the best position by shifting left to right while he waited for the officer to come back. His was the first appointment of the day but apparently, the woman's paperwork was scattered across various offices. When she returned, he sat with his right ankle resting on his left knee. She handed Tom a copy of his loan papers.

"The problem is that you've been late several times, so the bank has now requested full payment. As a matter of fact, you still haven't made your last payment due three weeks ago."

Tom was immediately annoyed by the way these people talked. Who was "the bank"? They made it sound like it was a person, some higher-up who made all the decisions for the peons they called customers. Tom refused to refer to it as 'The Bank'.

"Can't you talk to those people? I'll be able to pay the full amount in a few days. I'll be all set. As I explained, I'm going to receive a very large sum of money for the painting."

"It won't do any good. The loan has been called in and I don't think they can reverse that. A painting isn't cash you see. Is there any other guarantee?"

Tom saw a little opening, took his leg off his knee and sat up straight.

"I'm sure the people at the Metropolitan will confirm my story."

"That may be the case. But there are other issues. I see that you have depleted your savings account and you know yourself how your checking account looks. Considering interest and penalties, you will need to come up with a large payment quickly. And, Mr. Arden, don't forget your credit card situation. I'm sure they've called you already."

"I've talked to them," Tom lied. "I'll be all set with them on Monday. Really, you need to talk with the Metropolitan."

"Okay, let's get them on the phone. I'll talk with them."

Schroller had taken a drive early in the morning to LaGuardia Airport. Sitting in the parking lot, Schroller took his phone and clicked on the *Photos* icon and then on *Camera Roll*. He brought up the picture he took of Isabelle and choose the *MMS* option. He typed Tom's cell phone number and a short message. When he heard the sound that confirmed the message and picture were sent, he turned his phone off completely.

At the bank, Tom gave the telephone number to the bank officer. She made the call. Dr. Amado wasn't available and she left a short message with her name and telephone number.

"Sorry, I'll see what I can do after he calls. For now, your account is in collect status."

"I understand, but please call me as soon as you have talked with Dr. Amado and your people at the bank." Tom said, taking his phone.

Just as he was putting it in his pocket, it buzzed. He was hoping that Dr. Amado was calling him, but it was a text message and a picture from Schroller.

"Excuse me for a second," he said, clicking on the message. He stood up and read it: *Early afternoon today. Instructions to follow. Enjoy attachment.* Tom turned away from the desk and scrolled up to see a picture. He saw the lower part of Isabelle's face, her shoulder and the top of her left arm that had two red marks on it. He sat back down and his face turned white. He looked ill.

"Are you all right, Mr. Arden?" the woman asked.

"No, not really. I just got some very bad news. Can we pick up this conversation on Monday maybe? I need to go."

"Fine with me, Mr. Arden. Don't forget, you have until Monday."

"Thank you. I'll call you," Tom said, almost mechanically since his mind was on Isabelle and the picture he had just seen.

Tom walked toward his car with his hands in his pockets. He was shaking. After he unlocked his car, he looked at the picture again, his eyes fixed on the burn marks.

"Fucking bastard!" he yelled, as he remembered Isabelle's scream.

With tears in his eyes, he kicked the tires, swore and screamed at no one in particular.

"I can't believe this. Why is this happening? This guy leaves me no choice."

Tom jumped into his car and took off. He wasn't headed anywhere in particular so once he realized that, he slowed down. He came to a small park and pulled to the side of the road. He dialed Marco.

"Marco, he's torturing Isabelle! I have proof! I have the picture!" he yelled.

"What pic . . ." Marco started to ask.

"Of Isabelle. He's fucking torturing her like I told you yesterday. He just sent me a text message with a picture. She has like burn marks on her arm. It makes me sick just looking at it."

"I'm really sorry, Tom. The police are going all out trying to find her, believe me. Was there anything else in the message?"

"Yeah, he's going to send me instructions on where to meet. I just want to pay the guy to make him go away, you know."

"Tom! C'mon. It's the painting, stupid. He doesn't want anything else. How many times do we need to go over this?"

"Yeah? I thought everyone could be bought. I thought you were going to talk to O'Grady about my plan to draw Schroller to the auction."

"That's not going to happen, Tom."

"Screw it," Tom yelled and threw his phone on the passenger seat.

Tom unlocked the door to his store, walked in, and slammed it shut. He threw his keys on the desk and opened the cabinet above the credenza behind his desk and stared at the bottles of booze. Which one to grab? Before he could make up his mind, he closed the cabinet door without taking out a bottle. He took off his jacket and put it on his chair. He grabbed his phone out of a pocket and stared at it, as if willing for Schroller to call him with the details of the drop.

"C'mon you bastard. Call me! Let's get it over with," he mumbled. After about ten minutes of just sitting there, he put his phone back in his jacket pocket. With tears welling up in his eyes, he suddenly flung his arms across his desk, knocking things down to the ground. He broke the vase and a lamp. He swore at everything and everybody that came to his mind. He was about to do a final swipe when he saw the statue and paused. He stopped the motion to clear the entire desk. He had just thought about something and grabbed his phone.

"This is Tom Arden at the art store. I'm closing my store for a few weeks starting this weekend. I suggest you pick up the statue right now. How about it?"

Tom listened to the client.

"Okay, I'll see you in a few minutes."

He slowly picked up the pieces of the broken vase.

"You're an asshole, Tom. A loser."

He cleaned up the rest of the stuff on the floor by pushing things with his foot under his desk.

"Damn vase. There goes sixty grand, damn it."

He dropped into his desk chair and held the statue for a while. He sighed deeply and put it down on the desk. He shook his head and went to the back room looking for a box. He found one that would do and walked back into the storefront, just as the client walked in.

"Well, that was quick," Tom said, almost startled.

"It sounded like I needed to do this today."

The client sat down and Tom hesitated for a second.

"I'm sorry but I do have to tell you that there's been a change in price."

"What do you mean? You just called me and I rushed over. I got the money. All twenty five thousand of it," the man said.

Tom held the statue and looked at it. He grabbed the box.

"Thirty thousand and it's yours."

"But we agreed on twenty five."

"I've got another buyer and he's willing to pay thirty."

"That may be, but you called me and we agreed on twenty five."

"I'll take your twenty five today and you can pay me the rest tomorrow," Tom answered.

The man took a step back and Tom put the statue in the box. At that moment, Marco walked into the store. Both the client and Tom looked over their shoulder to Marco, who in turn stared at Tom with piercing eyes and in total disbelief.

"Sorry, I didn't mean to intrude," he said, already turning and ready to leave.

"No, you didn't, I was . . ." Tom tried, but Marco interrupted him.

"I'm sorry. In more ways than one," he said and left, slamming the door shut.

The client stared at Tom who put up his finger.

"Hold on for a second," he said and ran to the door.

Outside he looked for Marco, but only saw the back of Marco's car disappear down the street. Dejected, he walked back into the store.

"Damn. So much for that."

The client was still standing by the desk.

"So then, are you sticking with the thirty grand?"

Tom walked around his desk and sat down. He closed the box and put it on the ground.

"Sorry, but I'm not selling it after all."

"What? How can you say that? First you're selling it for twenty five, suddenly it's thirty and then it's not for sale? What kind of store is this?" the man asked loudly.

"That's the way it is. I'm sorry," is all Tom could say. His mind was suddenly on other things.

"I'm sorry too. Was that your other customer that just walked in?"

"Uh, yeah. I'm just not ready to sell it. There's an issue with it which I don't want to get into right now."

"Well, you've certainly wasted my time."

"Sorry about that," Tom said and the client walked out. The door slammed shut for the third time in a half hour.

Marco was speeding away, without any particular destination in mind. He just wanted to be away from Tom. Clearly pissed off, he slammed his hand onto his steering wheel.

"I can't believe that guy," he said out loud.

He drove a few more minutes and pulled off into a fast food place and parked. He pulled out his phone and looked at the last dialed number. He pushed it away and dialed O'Grady.

"Anything going on at your end?" Marco asked.

"Well, you're right about that NYU professor being kidnapped. A graduate student has confirmed that the man he saw entering the building late last night was Schroller. He identified him from the picture."

"Like I said, with the painting as the connection, it had to be him."

"I've put extra people on the team and we're on it 24/7."

"That's good news. I'll keep looking too for the sake of the woman and the professor, but I'm afraid we've got a problem with Tom."

"How so?"

"He'll come up with an excuse not to sacrifice his damn painting. I know how he works."

"But there's nothing to lose. I talked to Dr. Amado about an hour ago, and he said the painting may be a forgery. It's basically worthless."

"Wait a minute. Did he say why or how he found that out?"

"No, he just said that there were suddenly doubts."

"And he didn't say why?"

"No, that's all he really said."

Marco paused for a few seconds.

"He does know that Stockton was kidnapped, right?"

"I didn't mention it, but now I get it."

"Hell, I should have figured this out last night. I get it now! I've got to go. I'll call you later."

It was quiet in Tom's store after his client had just stormed out. He understood the man's reaction. He had been treated badly. First he was told the price went up and then he wasn't even able to buy the statue at all. What kind of dealer am I, Tom wondered. Of course, Marco's showing up had changed the deal. Selling the statue hadn't really been on his mind, but he had to do something and needed money. He felt powerless. He couldn't do anything to help Isabelle. Selling the statue was an opportunity to do something. Marco obviously saw him with the client and the statue. He knew the conclusion Marco had made, and the way Marco had left was upsetting. Most likely Marco would be done helping him and he would have to make the drop by himself. The auction surely was a pipe dream now.

Lost in thought, Tom taped the box shut with the statue in it, and put it in on a table. When the phone rang, he answered without looking at the number, ready for an earful from Marco.

"Yeah, I'm listening," he said.

"Mr. Arden? What's wrong? This is Dr. Amado."

"I'm sorry. It has been a tough and terrible day. Nobody's probably told you, but the guy that kidnapped Isabelle is torturing her."

"What? That's insane," Dr. Amado said, raising his voice. "I am really sorry about this whole ordeal. I talked to the police earlier, so I knew they hadn't found Isabelle yet."

"Don't I know . . . This is so unfair. Anyway, I need to talk to you about the painting."

"That's exactly what I was calling you about."

"Oh?"

"Yes, I'm afraid I have some disappointing news. I'm afraid the painting may not be a Rembrandt after all . . ."

Tom's eyes widened and his jaw dropped open.

"But I thought it was certain! You told me yourself! The Dutch expert said so! What happened?"

"I understand you're quite upset, Mr. Arden. We can talk about it when you come to pick up the painting."

"I don't get it," Tom said. "Is it still an old painting?"

"I'm afraid it's one of the best forgeries."

"Then why would the kidnapper be after a worthless painting?"

"Maybe worthless in terms of money, but some people are very sentimental when it comes to art, regardless of the value it has on the market."

"I just can't believe this. It's bad enough that Isabelle was kidnapped because of it, but now it has no value, so now I lose out on a financially stable future."

"In any case, Mr. Metzer at Sotheby's is aware of the situation. Again, I'm sorry."

"Me too," Tom said and hung up, staring blankly in front of him.

CHAPTER 34

Friday Mid-morning

TOM HAD BEEN drinking and was holding the Johnny Walker bottle and a glass. He poured another glass as he looked at the clock. It was barely 10:30 a.m.

"Hell, it's five o'clock somewhere and life starts at five. Every day!"

He took another big gulp, sat down in his chair and put his feet on the table. His phone had rung several times already, but he didn't answer 800 numbers. It rang again, and assuming it was the credit card company, he mumbled to himself.

"Screw'em. I'm only waiting for my drop call. Got plenty of time to pick up that worthless piece of shit of a painting," he said with a distinctive slur.

"Oops, probably had a little too much," he said, putting the bottle down. He leaned back and closed his eyes. He must have dozed off for a few minutes, only to suddenly jerk up, swinging his feet off the desk. He realized that Schroller hadn't called yet for the drop and it was 11 a.m. Having had a few drinks made him bolder and less afraid of being berated by Marco, so he called him.

"Marco, Tom here. Now don't be mad."

"What do you want, Tom?"

"Listen, man," Tom said, still slurring his speech. "Things are really fucked up."

"You're telling me? You're screwed, boy."

"You have no fucking clue. Isabelle has been tortured and the painting is a fake. So what's left? All I can do is give him the junk and get Isabelle back, right?"

"Go for it."

"I can't do it myself. We had already decided that."

"Sober up, Tom. You can handle Schroller."

"I don't trust that German. You're the cop. I think you should do the drop anyway."

"Ex-cop. Our deal is off."

"C'mon. I need you," Tom said, rubbing his forehead. "My dad would have wanted you to help me . . . ."

Marco hesitated to answer.

"You're a son of a bitch."

"You promised my dad more than just stopping by, didn't you?"

Marco sighed heavily and walked to his car.

"Where are you?" he asked warily, starting the engine.

"At the store. Where else?"

"Get some coffee and sober up."

"Thanks," Tom whispered, hung up and closed his eyes again.

Marco parked in front of Tom's Porsche. He actually blocked him in so that whatever might happen, Tom would not be able to just take off in his car. Through the window he saw Tom behind his desk, just sitting there taking a nap. He couldn't believe it. He wondered how much he had to drink. Walking inside he could even smell the whiskey. The bottle was on the table and an empty glass was lying on its side on the desk. Just as he was about to say something he saw the same box he had seen earlier. It was now sitting on a table and it was taped shut. He returned his attention to Tom.

"What the hell are you doing?" he asked loudly, sweeping Tom's feet off the desk.

Tom woke up suddenly and panicked until he saw it was Marco. He was momentarily confused.

"I told you to sober up! You've got work to do," Marco said, pushing a Starbucks coffee in his face.

Tom focused and grabbed the coffee.

"Ah, you! Didn't think you'd really come back."

"Just sober up."

"Working on it. I didn't have any coffee here. So, are you ready to deal with that German bastard? He's going to call any minute."

"Show me that picture he sent."

Tom handed his phone to Marco who found the picture. Tom drank some coffee and coughed repeatedly while Marco looked at the picture.

"So, tell me about my dad and you."

"There's not much to tell other than what I told you already."

"Yes, but you left out the part where you promised him something, right?"

Marco looked at the picture again.

"Why do I feel like you're blackmailing me, dammit? I've got good reason to leave you in your own mess. I can't trust you and you're better off with the police."

"What do you mean you can't trust me? I've cleaned up my act. I've tried to set things right with some customers. You think I sold that statue. Well, you're wrong! I didn't."

"Looked like it to me."

Tom pointed at the box on the table.

"Nope, there it is. So, I'm not so bad after all, right?"

"I'm only here to see you get sobered up so you can go and make the drop."

"I told you I can't do this even if the cops are watching it. I failed the first time."

Marco fell silent for a while and paced back and forth in front of the desk.

"C'mon. I'll owe you . . ." Tom tried again.

"You already owe me as it is. But that's not the point."

"I still need your help," Tom pleaded, taking another big gulp of coffee.

Marco stood still and took a deep breath. He had come here with the intention of telling Tom to grow up, but instead he felt pity for him. He looked Tom straight in the eyes.

"I'll help you out with this drop and that's it!"

"Great. I really appreciate it," Tom said, and sat down again, relieved that he wouldn't have to face Schroller again.

Tom's phone rang while Marco still had it in his hand. He showed the caller ID to Tom, who quickly recognized it.

"It's him," Tom whispered. "You take it."

"Hello?" Marco asked.

"Who are you?" Schroller demanded to know when he didn't recognize the voice.

"I'm Marco. I'm an associate of Tom's."

"Is Tom there?"

Marco switched the phone to loudspeaker and put his finger across his lips.

"He's not here right now. He told me to take your instructions."

"I need *him* to make a delivery," Schroller insisted.

"He is too depressed to deliver anything, especially the painting."

"Does he know that the painting is basically worthless, like I predicted? This is going to be an easy thing, right?"

"Yes, where do I meet you?"

"I'd rather have Tom come to meet me."

"Sorry buddy. Like I said, he's in no shape to do that. He's a little under the weather."

"What is that supposed to mean?" Schroller asked.

Marco realized that the German didn't understand the expression. Maybe it was better to clarify.

"He's drunk so if you want him, you'll have to wait until tomorrow, I'm sure he can bring the painting then. Anyway, how's his girlfriend Isabelle?

"She's okay for now."

"Put her on the phone."

"She's not here."

"Bring her to the drop place," Marco said, looking at his watch, wanting to keep Schroller talking as long a possible.

"Be at the corner of 14th and Union Square at 1:30 p.m. Walk into the deli and ask for the package for Mr. Rembrandt. In it you'll find a phone. Wait there outside and I will call you when I see you. Wrap the painting in brown paper," Schroller said.

"Will Isabelle be there?" Marco tried again, but the signal was lost. He looked at Tom and raised his eyebrows.

"Let me call the precinct. I'm sure they were able to locate where his call came from," Marco said.

"Forget it," Tom said. "This call wasn't from his cell phone. That's a totally different number."

"Well, let's get this over with."

"What do you want me to do?"

"Get some more coffee at the diner. I'll call O'Grady on my way to the Met."

"So, I sit there and wait?"

"Yes, but first call Amado. Tell him I'm picking up the painting in about 45 minutes. It's essential I have it. Got it?"

"Yeah, I got it."

Marco walked to the door and turned around.

"If you have a problem reaching Amado, call me."

"Hold on," Tom said grabbing his jacket and his keys. "I'm leaving for the diner right now."

Marco held the door and waited for Tom who finished the coffee Marco had brought.

Tom felt like he was becoming a regular at the diner. He found an empty booth in the corner and ordered a black coffee and a piece of pie. He called Dr. Amado. By now he wasn't slurring his words, but his head was still buzzing. He was sure the waitress had noticed something but she didn't say anything.

Dr. Amado answered right away.

"Dr. Amado? This is Tom Arden again."

"Yes, Tom, anything on Isabelle?"

"Unfortunately not. I am calling about the painting."

"What do you want me to do with it?

"Get it ready so that we can exchange it for Isabelle."

"I understand."

"So, please have it packaged up as simply as possible in brown paper wrapping. Marco will pick it up in about thirty minutes. Can you have it near the entrance?"

"No problem, Tom, I'll have it packaged and ready for him.

Tom thought Dr. Amado sounded as disappointed as he was. Given the importance and the value if it had been an original Rembrandt, it was no surprise. In his gut, he had a feeling that there was something odd about this whole authentication process. On the one hand, all regular and traditional tests had shown it to be a Rembrandt. Then bringing this Dutch expert over was like saying 'we're just about sure, but want his blessing'. Perhaps it was all that scientific analysis that had revealed it to be a fraud, or perhaps the x-rays or something else. Any process where machines were involved bothered him. He hadn't known about that part of the process in the beginning, and when Dr. Amado told him, he had a bad feeling. He was tempted to say, "I told you so." Maybe he would next time when he saw Dr. Amado.

Tom finished the piece of pie and emptied his coffee cup. Almost immediately, the waitress came by and filled it up again. He thanked her, but his mind was mostly on the situation and what to do next. First, Isabelle had to be found. For the rest, well the painting wasn't going to get him any money, so his financial future was dismal with only bankruptcy on the horizon.

He stared outside, thinking how stupid he had been to throw the vase on the ground. He was sure Marco had noticed the shards on the floor under his desk, but thankfully he hadn't said anything about it. The vase had cost him a few thousand, not very much in the grand scheme of things. There was no way that one client was going to buy it as a Ming vase anyway. Not that he was going to tell Marco that it was a Qing dynasty vase. At least he wouldn't be tempted to cheat anyone with that one anymore. Now that the statue was no longer in the picture, he had nothing else going on. Tom had a feeling of total resignation. Once the bank took his inventory and he declared bankruptcy, he would have to start something else. But that was for later, first he had to get Isabelle back.

After the second cup of hot coffee, Tom was sweating. He picked a copy of the NY Post lying on a table next to his booth and started reading the headlines, although with little interest. A few pages into the paper, his phone rang and Tom saw it was Marco.

"Did you pick up the painting yet?"

"Just picked it up. The tracer is inside. I'm driving to Union Square."

"Okay. Good luck," Tom said and hung up.

Even though he knew it was going to upset him again, he decided to take another look at the picture of Isabelle. He brought it up and stared at the burn marks. He shook his head. He couldn't see her whole face which was a good thing. She must have been in enormous pain and maybe still was. His eyes wandered around the picture, away from Isabelle's arm. He noticed a small card on the table to the right of the picture. He put his finger and thumb together on the surface of his iPhone and enlarged the picture several times. Tom's heart skipped a beat. Clearly readable on the card, he saw a red number 6.

"A Motel 6! Damn, that's where she is!" he said out loud to himself. "Why didn't I look at that closer before?

He saved the picture to his phone and then clicked on *Camera Roll*. He enlarged the picture and studied everything in more detail but couldn't find anything else. He clicked on *Camera Roll* again to close the display and touched *Places* on the bottom of the display by mistake. He hadn't seen this feature before.

"What do we have here?" he mumbled.

The display showed a map of the North and South America. Several red pins were piled on top of each other in the New York area. He tried to enlarge the map and was surprised it worked. He finally ended up with a detailed map of Queens. There were two pins. When he touched the first pin, he saw that it was a location for five pictures. The other one indicated one single picture. Excitedly he clicked on the arrow next to the text and Isabelle's picture popped up.

"I know where you are, Isabelle," he said a bit louder.

He quickly went back to *Places* and enlarged the map to street level even more, keeping an eye on the one pin. And then, there it was, the street name and the approximate location on the street.

By now totally sober, Tom smiled.

"So that's where you are," he said, getting up. He threw a ten dollar bill on the counter and left.

CHAPTER 35

Friday Afternoon~1:30 PM

MARCO HAD A tough time finding a parking place and ended up in a parking garage just past 1:30 p.m. He would make it a point to remember to charge Tom after everything was settled. He hurried over to the store on 14th Street and asked for the Rembrandt package. It was a small box which he opened in the store. In it was a simple phone. He opened the flap and saw that it was fully charged. The moment he set foot outside the store, the phone rang.

"You're running late. You'll have to make up the time. Is that the painting you're carrying?" Schroller asked.

"Of course. Where are you?"

"Don't worry where I am. We've got quite a ways to go. Keep the phone opened and by your ear."

"I get it. What now?" Marco asked.

"Go into the subway station across the street and take the 5 Train to Astor Place."

Marco darted across the street and disappeared down the stairway of the subway.

Less than a hundred yards away, O'Grady and two of his men were watching Marco. When they saw him enter the subway station, O'Grady motioned a few men on the street to follow Marco down. He and the two men got into an unmarked car and waited to hear from the other men. Soon he got the call he was waiting for.

"He's on the 5, going south."

O'Grady ordered the two men to head in the same direction. After a few seconds he had confirmation of Marco's location through the tracking device in the package. Confident that they were following closely, O'Grady pushed on above ground. As long as they followed Marco and the painting, they were also following Schroller.

Marco took the short ride on the subway and got off at Astor Place. He looked around for Schroller. He was sure that if Schroller could control his movements, he had to be nearby. He was hoping that the tracking device worked.

Schroller was standing near the end of the platform. Undetected, he made his way up to street level. Once outside, he gave Marco his next instruction.

"Exit the subway and make your way to the 8th Street NYU station. Wait there for my instructions."

"Got it," Marco said as he walked up the escalator, followed by two detectives.

Schroller spotted them when they appeared on the street as they almost bumped into Marco who had stopped for a quick orientation. They each walked their own way but stopped after about twenty yards and looked at store windows. Schroller was familiar with that move and now had to make Marco execute the next step exactly like he had planned.

"Okay, let's shake the guys following you," he said.

"What do you want me to do?" Marco asked.

"Walk fast to the next station, about four blocks to your left. Then I want you to run down the stairs," Schroller ordered.

Marco made his way to the subway station and ran down the steps. The painting bumped into several people and Marco wondered what kind of damage was being done to it. Not that it mattered so much if this was a fake, but for a while now, he had this hunch that maybe this was real after all. What if it turned out that Stockton had been forced to call it a forgery? He had no proof of course, but the painting under his arm was worth millions and then any damage would be terrible. On the other hand, right now the painting was the bait to lure Schroller, nothing more. He hadn't mentioned his hunch to Amado because it may have made him doubt the forgery claim. In that case, he would have balked at giving the painting to him. He sure as hell hadn't told Tom either for the same reason. No, this was the only way he was willing to part with it and it was the only chance of getting Isabelle back.

Once he reached the first platform, he heard Schroller scream in the phone.

"Wait right there!"

Marco waited for five seconds and a train approached. Schroller barked into the phone again.

"Run to the north platform. You better make it fast!"

In a busy crowd, Marco ran a few more flights down. Schroller yelled to take the train that was arriving on the north platform. Marco made it just in time before the doors closed.

As the train pulled out of the station he saw two men running down the stairs. He wasn't too worried about having lost the two men since he still had the tracking device inside the package. Hopefully, it was working. Within a half a minute, Schroller was talking again. Marco held the phone close to his ear.

"Nice work."

"I just made it."

"I know. You're doing just fine. Now, get off at 23rd Street. You have 10 minutes."

Marco sat down and put the painting between his sore legs. He wasn't used to having to run up and down stairs like this and it felt good to take a break.

O'Grady heard from the men following Marco. They lost him. Luckily, O'Grady confirmed the direction the painting was traveling in, and they took the next train. With a subway map in his hand, he plotted the various stops and called for police backup at every station and to be on the lookout for Marco with the painting in a brown paper package. Near every station his driver slowed down briefly, but soon the train outran them. They drove as fast as possible following the underground track.

The Motel 6 was less than three miles from Tom's store, but with the Friday afternoon traffic it took longer than Tom had anticipated.

He ran a few lights and was going much too fast, at one point just missing a pedestrian crossing the street as he took a turn. If he wasn't sober before, he was definitely with it now. The adrenaline rush and the excitement of being able to free Isabelle were his driving forces. His Porsche finally came to a screeching halt in front of the lobby of the motel. From the passenger seat he quickly took the police photo of Schroller and ran inside.

There was nobody behind the desk and he looked around desperately. There wasn't even a bell to get someone's attention.

"Hello, anyone here?" he asked loud enough for someone in the back office to hear.

A man stuck his head around the corner where he was filling a coffee thermos.

"I'm the manager. May I help you?" he asked.

"Do you know what room this guy is staying in?" Tom asked, holding Schroller's picture up.

"I can't tell you that, sir."

"Really, it's a matter of life and death. This guy has kidnapped my girlfriend and has her in his room."

"Call the cops."

"You don't understand. The cops are trying to get him when he collects the ransom. Hurry."

The manager returned to his desk and walked by Tom. He could smell Tom's breath as he was talking.

"As I said, I can't help you. You've been drinking. I can smell it through the coffee. Find another place to sleep it off."

"I'm not drunk! You've got to help me!"

"Call the cops," the man said again and walked away to the back office.

Tom couldn't believe that the man wouldn't help him and yelled in the direction of the back office that he was going to find it himself. He ran outside and started walking by the rooms on the ground floor. He called O'Grady.

"Detective O'Grady? This is Tom."

"Hey, Tom, listen we're busy here tracking your painting and Schroller."

"This is more important. I'm at the motel where he's holding Isabelle!

"How did you find that?"

"I used the location feature on my iPhone from the picture of Isabelle he had sent. I didn't know it could do that. Anyway, the guy at the motel won't let me get to the room. Can you send a cop?"

"Wait for a patrol car. I'll have someone there in a minute. Where are you?"

"Motel 6 on 87th in Queens."

"Stay there and let the cops handle it!"

"Okay, but have them get here quickly. Thanks," Tom said and ended the call.

He started looking through the windows of the rooms on the ground floor. Only five had the curtains closed all the way. Three of them had *No Smoking* signs on them. He figured that if Isabelle was on the ground floor, it would have to be in one of the rooms where the curtains were closed. The two rooms without the *No Smoking* signs had a *Do not Disturb* sign hanging from the door handle. She had to be in one of these, Tom figured. He jiggled both door handles. Both doors were locked. He knocked on the first door and called Isabelle's name. Nothing. The same thing happened at the second door. He realized that if she was in there, Schroller had made sure she couldn't make any noise.

Tom ran back to the reception area where the manager was standing behind the desk again. When he saw Tom enter, he frowned and grabbed the phone, ready to dial. Tom didn't mind him calling the cops. He just hoped the cops O'Grady was sending would get there first.

"Listen, the cops are on their way. But I figure she's either in 124 or 125. C'mon, we don't have time to lose."

"Maybe, but I'm still calling," the manager said shaking his head.

At that moment a police car arrived, briefly sounding its siren as it pulled up next to Tom's car. Two cops, a man and a woman, got out and Tom ran outside.

"You Tom?" the male cop asked.

"Yeah. Get the guy in there to tell you which room the kidnapper got. It's either 124 or 125 I think."

"My name is Frank. I'll find out," the cop said and walked inside.

"I'm Joanna," the female cop said. "Follow me. O'Grady said the kidnapper's not here, but he may have an accomplice, so stay well back," she said, walking toward the rooms.

As they neared room 124, she pulled her gun and held it up with both hands.

"The kidnapper is collecting the ransom in Manhattan," Tom said.

"We were briefed by our captain. Let's hope he's acting alone. That should make this part easy."

The other cop and the manager, key in hand, came running behind them and they stopped short of 124. Frank motioned to Tom and the manager to stay where they were. He took several steps forward and knocked on the door, backing off immediately. There was no answer and both cops held their guns ready. Frank took the key, unlocked the door and opened it a little. He then stood back.

"Police! Anyone here?" he asked, but all was quiet in the dark room.

Joanna, put her hand around the door opening and turned on the lights. Together with Frank, she rushed in checking the bedroom, the bathroom and the closet.

"Nobody here," she called out and Tom and the manager walked in. Tom seemed dumbfounded and looked at the manager.

"He did have this room, right?"

"Yes, this is the room he paid for."

Tom looked around, then saw the ashtray.

"See this," he pointed out. "There are little cigar stubs from the stuff he smokes."

"So, he did stay here," Joanna said, looking around the room for other hints.

Tom was the first to think about the adjoining room when he noticed the connecting door to room 125.

"Who's in that room?" he asked the manager.

"That's someone else's room," he said.

"Open it up," Frank demanded.

"There may be someone in there," the manager objected.

The cop knocked on the door and thought he heard something, so he knocked again. This time he was sure that he heard a moan.

"Open it," he ordered.

The manager unlocked the door. The other inside door was unlocked. The cops pushed it open and in the dim light they immediately saw a man sitting on the ground, tied to a bed.

Tom ran to him while the cops checked the rest of the room. He slowly started pulling the tape off Stockton's mouth, but the Joanna came over and ripped it off quickly.

"Much easier. Short pain."

Stockton, nevertheless, grimaced in pain.

"Where's Isabelle?" Tom asked right away.

"The kidnapper left with her a few hours ago. I'm Dr. Stockton."

"Did he say where he was taking her," Joanna asked while her partner cut the ties from Stockton's wrists and ankles.

"No. Does anyone have a phone? I've got to make a call right away."

Tom handed him his phone while Stockton got up.

"Thanks," he said, pushing the digits on the keypad. His hand was shaking while he held the phone by his ear.

"Dr. Amado? Stockton. Listen, disregard what I told you yesterday morning. The painting is a genuine Rembrandt! I was forced to lie by the guy that kidnapped the woman, Isabelle, and me. I'll explain later. I've got to go now."

"You mean my painting is a Rembrandt for sure?" Tom asked excitedly.

"Ah, you're Tom. Yes, it is. There is no doubt," Stockton said sitting down on the edge of the bed.

"Oh, shit," Tom said. "We're about to hand the painting to Schroller, your kidnapper."

He took his phone back from Stockton and called Marco. There was no answer, so he called O'Grady.

"We got Stockton," he said.

"That's great work, Tom! How about Isabelle?"

"He took her with him."

"I doubt she's with him. It would make picking up the painting too complicated."

"Listen, don't let Marco give the painting to Schroller. It's a real Rembrandt. We need to lure him to the auction."

"Why?" O'Grady asked. "We're tracking the painting and Schroller. He's our only link to Isabelle. We don't want to jeopardize her safety."

"He knows about the auction and if you lure him to Sotheby's, there's no way he would be able to get back to wherever he's holding her. He would have to hurry there."

"When is the auction scheduled?"

"In about an hour."

"I think we can do it. I think you may be right. Either he shows up there with Isabelle, or without her. In any case, we can easily catch him there. Unfortunately, I doubt we can reach Marco before the drop. In any case, why don't you head for the auction? I'll call you as soon as I have more information.

"Thanks. I hope you reach Marco and convince him to go to Sotheby's immediately. Make sure you have your men there because Schroller will show up there. I'm sure of it." Tom said.

CHAPTER 36

Friday Afternoon—2 PM

M ARCO SURFACED FROM the subway station on 23rd Street and waited for further instructions. His own phone had been ringing but by the time he juggled the painting and the other phone, he was too late to answer. He listened to the new phone, but Schroller was making him wait. Actually, Schroller, leaning against a black limousine parked near the subway station entrance, was not only looking at Marco, but also at the surrounding area. He didn't spot any cops or undercover people. He was satisfied. He talked into his phone again.

"Almost there. Stay on this phone and forget about your own phone!"

"I'm not making any calls," Marco said, looking around trying to find Schroller. He couldn't spot him.

"Keep it that way and start walking north on Broadway until you come to a bookstore on the left. Wait there."

As soon as Marco started walking again, his own phone rang again. This time he was ready, and not expecting to hear from Schroller any time soon, he answered.

"Yes, quickly!"

"Tom found Stockton! The painting's the real thing and he doesn't want you to hand it over. He wants to lure Schroller to the auction," O'Grady said.

"Don't like the idea. We need to find Isabelle."

"We're searching, believe me. Cancel the drop. You're on 23rd and Broadway, right?"

"Yes,"

"Stay there. A car will pick you up. Tell the cop to drive straight to Sotheby's. Tom's plan may work out," O'Grady said and hung up.

Marco put his phone back in his pocket, not happy with the change in plans, even if he did have a multi million dollar painting under his arm. He heard Schroller yelling in the other phone.

"Who were you talking to?" he demanded to know.

"The cops," Marco said, standing still at the corner, scouting the area for his adversary.

"I better not see any. Why are you standing still? Keep moving."

"Slight problem. I can't give this package to you if you can't give me Isabelle."

"You will get her soon enough after you leave the painting."

Marco saw a cop car with flashing lights approaching him and slowing down. He waved at the cop.

"Watch me disappear, asshole," he said waving his hand around at wherever Schroller might have been hiding.

"You can't," Schroller yelled as Marco got into the police car.

"See you at the auction in about a half hour if you want the painting!"

Schroller swore in German and got into the back seat of the waiting limousine. The driver pulled into traffic slowly, away from several police cars converging on the corner of 23rd and Broadway.

Tom was driving toward Manhattan with Stockton sitting next to him. The cops were in front of them clearing the lane on the expressway using their flashing lights and siren. They were in a hurry to reach downtown and get to Sotheby's. Tom and Stockton had been talking about Schroller and how he had tortured Isabelle.

"Think, Dr. Stockton, did he give any clues as to where he was taking her?" Tom asked, tailgating the police car in front of him.

"No, he dragged her out and told me to sit tight, as if I was going to go anywhere."

"Did he say anything leading up to leaving with her?"

"He kept saying that you had the easiest job, to hand over the worthless painting. By the way, I'm surprised you didn't find out that it is a forgery until this morning," Stockton wondered.

"I think people wanted to keep it from me. Anyway, what else? There's got to be something. Did he talk to her yesterday? Think!" Tom insisted.

"Wait," Stockton said. "At one point he got very ambitious. He talked about her getting a few paintings from the museum's storage rooms. In return he'd let her go after he got the Rembrandt and the other paintings."

"What did she say?"

"She said he was dreaming if he thought she'd ever go near the museum with him."

"What did he say then?"

"He just laughed."

Tom thought about that for a while.

"It sounded like he wanted to go to the museum again with Isabelle."

"That would be crazy, with all the cameras and the guards."

"That's what bothers me."

"Once he has the Rembrandt he'd have to move very fast to get more paintings and not get caught."

"That's right. You got it. She's got to be close to the Met, because he'd have to get away quickly."

"I still don't see how he could get in."

"He got her out, so he knows how to get in."

"Do they know how he got out?"

"The loading dock! That's it!" Tom said excitedly and immediately sped the car up even more, passing the patrol car when the lane next to them opened up a little. He then cut back into the lane in front of the patrol car.

The cops looked surprised, but Tom and Stockton gave them the thumbs up, assuming they'd interpret it to mean they were okay on their own from here. However, the cops followed them toward Manhattan.

"I've got to call Marco," Tom said. "He's the one who's making the drop."

Marco answered right away.

"Yes, Tom, I just got to Sotheby's. I'll give the painting to Dr. Amado."

"Whew! Glad you got that message."

"I sure hope this works, Tom. Good work on finding Stockton though."

"I wish it had been Isabelle, but I think I know where he's keeping her."

"Where?"

"Somewhere at the Met, I'm sure of it."

"Do you want me to send the cops?"

"No need. We've got a few following us. We're already in midtown. You and the cops look out for Schroller. You know he'll come after the painting there."

"I hope you're right. O'Grady just got here."

"I'll call you when we find her. Just get Schroller," Tom said and hung up. With the cops on his back bumper, he drove as fast as he could, obeying the traffic laws.

CHAPTER 37

Friday Afternoon-2:30 PM

MARCO HAD JUST handed the package to Dr. Amado who rushed the painting inside the building with a guard at his side. Marco had assured him that the painting was okay, although he had bumped into several people and doors with it. Any damage would be to the frame which wasn't the original frame anyway, Tom had told him before.

As he stood outside near the entrance, a cop car pulled up in front of the building. Marco recognized the men and asked them to take a position on the other side of the street. They made a quick U-turn and parked. O'Grady and two detectives were inside taking a look at the layout of the building and Marco was waiting for them to return. It was Dr. Amado who came back first.

"So, any word on Isabelle?"

"Tom called me a little while ago. He thinks she's locked up somewhere at the Met. He's got a few cops with him to look for her. I think Dr. Stockton is with him also."

"I'll call our head of security right away."

"That's a good idea. By the way, where are all the people. Don't hundreds of people come to an auction like this?"

"It's a very private auction."

"I see. Go ahead you don't want to miss it. Good luck. We'll take care of Schroller when he shows up," Marco said.

He checked his gun and scanned the area. Within a few minutes O'Grady's team came back outside as a few more patrol cars pulled up. The cops lined the sidewalk in front of the building. Most of their cars were parked on the other side of the street. O'Grady looked at the men and gave his last instructions.

"All right men. You know what he looks like. Third time is the charm. Let's get him," he said. He turned to Marco.

"You saved that painting just in time."

"And I wasn't going to take your call. I was sure he was watching me and with that awkward package, there is no way I could have used my weapon if he had threatened me."

"Well, the painting's safe. Let's hope he shows up. When's that auction supposed to start?"

"In about fifteen minutes," Marco said, looking at his watch. "Haven't seen many people, but apparently it's by invitation only and private."

O'Grady's phone rang and he answered. He listened for a moment and said goodbye.

"My men are almost to the museum. They'll keep me up to date on finding Isabelle."

Marco nodded and lit a cigarette. He moved away from the entrance to keep the smoke from bothering anyone. O'Grady was talking to one of the detectives and everyone was scanning the area for Schroller. A limo had just dropped off a couple, presumably for the auction, and they walked right in, without even looking at the show of force near the entrance.

A few minutes later, another black stretch limo pulled up. This one drew a little more attention because it had two Dutch flags on the hood. The chauffeur walked around the car and opened the door for a tall, dark haired man who wore a dark overcoat and gloves. He had an earring in one ear only and had a rather large mustache. His sunglasses made him look like someone important who didn't want to be recognized. O'Grady and Marco looked at him briefly and then scanned the street again as the limo pulled away.

The man was smoking and took one last drag before going up the stairs. He threw the stub down on the sidewalk and ground it with his heel. He went up the steps as a doorman held the door open and he walked in.

O'Grady had noticed the man throw the stub down and shook his head. Standing next to Marco, he couldn't resist making a comment.

"You know, we should ticket these rich guys for littering."

Marco smiled, not knowing what O'Grady was talking about. O'Grady pointed at the stub left on the sidewalk and Marco suddenly froze. He quickly stepped down and bent over to pick up what was left of the stub. Getting up, he held the stub under his nose, but he already knew whose it was. He ran up the steps to the front door as he yelled to O'Grady.

"It's him. I'm sure. He's inside."

Marco ran through the lobby looking for Schroller.

"Was it the guy from the limo?" Marco asked O'Grady who was right behind him.

"Yes, he's got dark hair and a mustache and was wearing a dark overcoat," O'Grady yelled back.

O'Grady had drawn his gun out and followed Marco who was looking for a man fitting the description. There were only a few people in the lobby. The doors to the gallery area and offices were closed. Not seeing Schroller in the lobby, Marco opened one of the doors and caught a glimpse of man with a dark coat, just rounding the corner. O'Grady followed Marco and alerted his men inside the building to be on the lookout. Marco and O'Grady ran to the spot where they last saw Schroller. They carefully peeked around the corner, but the short hallway was empty. There were two doors. One of them was to an exhibition room, the other a meeting room. They carefully opened the door to the exhibition room. A guard stood just inside the room.

"Did you see a man just come in, dressed in a dark overcoat, black hair and a mustache?" O'Grady asked flashing his badge.

The old guard, not sure what was going on, was flustered.

"Yeah, sure, uh . . . he went that way," he stammered, pointing to the opening to a room off the main exhibition room. It had no doors.

"Thanks," O'Grady said. "Get these people out of here, now!"

Marco was already at the corner of the room and drew his gun. When O'Grady nodded, they both dashed around the corner into the smaller exhibition room.

"Stop! Raise your hands," O'Grady yelled at the man standing in front of a painting with his back toward the entrance.

The man raised his hands and slowly turned toward Marco and O'Grady while a woman, also dressed in black, appeared from behind a side panel.

"What's going on? Who are you? Why are you pointing your guns at my husband," she demanded to know.

The man had now turned around completely. Marco realized that this was not Schroller. The man didn't even have a mustache.

Tom parked his car near the loading dock next to a delivery truck. A second later, the cops pulled up behind him and got out in a hurry.

"What are we doing here?" Frank asked.

"I think Isabelle is being hidden here at the museum."

"Okay, let's check it out," the cop said as they all walked up the side steps to the metal door.

Tom tried the handle, but the door was locked. He pounded with his fist on the door, hoping someone inside would hear. With a delivery truck outside, there were bound to be people around. He was surprised when there was no reaction.

"We can walk around through the entrance and get back here from the other side of the door," Joanna suggested.

"Wait," Tom said, as he dialed Dr. Amado's number. "I'll have someone alert security inside."

Dr. Amado answered after the first ring. He recognized Tom's number.

"Yes, Tom. Did you find Isabelle?"

"Not yet. We're outside the loading dock. Can you have someone open the door from the inside? I know Isabelle's here somewhere. Hurry!" Tom said.

"I already called security. They were waiting at the main entrance. I'll send someone over right now," Dr. Amado said and hung up.

Stockton knocked on the door to make sure the guard would know where they were. Marco was pacing back and forth on the platform checking his watch. Suddenly the door opened and a guard let them in.

The loading dock area looked like a small warehouse for a packing company. There were boxes, crates and blankets stacked along the walls. There was a ladder standing alongside one wall and next to it a wide bulletin board covered with flyers of exhibitions and various schedules. There was only one office in the back and that was empty. One door gave access to a hallway with more offices. Tom and Stockton ran from office to office while the cops were doing a more thorough job, looking in closets, large cabinets and underneath desks. They all came up empty. Tom ran back to the guard who was standing near another door.

"Are there any other offices here?"

"No, that's it. The rest is just storage space. I'm not assigned to this area, but I think that's all there is," the guard said, spreading his arms wide.

Tom was puzzled. Maybe he had it wrong after all. He was sure Schroller would have thought he had easier access here, and he could have gotten in using Isabelle's access card. Somehow he had gotten in without the cops standing at the corner of the building seeing him. Then he noticed a camera in the hallway. He ran back to the loading area and looked around until he spotted a camera there as well. He stepped back outside and right away saw a camera on the side of the building.

"Do these cameras record everything today?" he asked the guard.

"Yes, I'm sure they do," the guard replied.

"We need to see the DVR now," Frank demanded, understanding where Tom was going.

They all went back to the hallway and followed the security guard up the stairs to the second floor.

Marco apologized to the husband and wife and quickly ran back to the hallway. Schroller must have gone into the area of the building where the offices were. O'Grady checked with two of his men over by the auction room but they hadn't seen a man fitting the description.

"Has the auction started?" O'Grady asked.

"No sir, not that we know. It's all quiet here and we haven't seen anyone enter or leave this way."

O'Grady frowned and hung up. He and Marco entered a long hallway with a multitude of doors on either side. As they checked what was behind each door, people were at work at their desks. There was no sign of Schroller as they pushed on toward the end of the hallway. The last door was ajar and Marco pushed it open. The open area they came into looked more like a plush waiting room with overstuffed chairs all around, small tables with art magazines and one large coffee table. There was nobody in the room, but Marco thought he heard a door close in a small kitchen that opened up into the room. He ran over quickly and was sure he had caught a glimpse of Schroller this time. One of the detectives who followed Marco, pushed the door open and quickly stepped aside, holding his gun ready.

Schroller turned around the moment the door opened and started shooting. The detective stepped in, the moment the gunfire stopped, probably figuring that Schroller had moved on. He had his gun ready, but Schroller was waiting for him. He shot the detective who collapsed in the doorway. Marco fired blindly to where he thought Schroller was standing, holding his gun around the corner. Not hearing anything anymore, Marco took his turn to step through the doorway. Schroller had opened a door at the end of a hallway. Marco fired right away, but Schroller fired one more shot before dashing into another room, and shot Marco. The shot was off the mark and the bullet hit Marco's leg. Marco slowly fell to the ground next to the detective who was lying on the floor, bleeding heavily from a spot below his shoulder. Marco and the detective now both blocked the doorway. Schroller was gone.

O'Grady and the cops came too late to help and they took care of the detective first.

"Are you going to be okay?" O'Grady asked.

"Yes, fine. Hurry. He went through the door straight ahead at the end of the hallway," Marco said while a cop helped him out of the doorway into the hallway. He was sitting and holding his leg tight to stop the bleeding.

Once in the other room, Schroller put his handgun in his belt and pulled a machine gun with an extra large clip from the inside of the long overcoat. He disappeared into yet another room. He had studied the layout carefully the day before and knew that there was more than one entrance to the auction room. He calmly went past two more offices and took the stairwell to the second floor. He couldn't believe his luck. He saw no cops or guards and decided to take a look at the main entrance to the auction room first. Looking carefully around the corner, he saw two cops in front of the big double door. He smiled. If they were waiting for him, they'd never see him. They had no idea how smart he was. Even though he wasn't nervous, he jumped when suddenly he heard someone announcing the Rembrandt auction. He was sure it was coming from the auction room, and he couldn't believe how loud it was. The bidding started at five million dollars. Going to plan B and the alternative route, Schroller smiled again.

"Overpriced painting. Suckers," he mumbled to himself, a bit surprised that the auction was going on, even though they must have heard the shooting.

CHAPTER 38

Friday Afternoon—3 PM

T OM WAS TERRIBLY frustrated, having failed in his search, but he had a fraction of hope left for the DVR to show something. In the security room, they started their search with the recording from 10:30 that morning. Stockton had estimated when Schroller and Isabelle had left, and that was about the time they could have gotten to the museum. If this is where they went, Stockton had said.

The video picture from the camera outside the loading dock looked as if it was a stationary picture. Nothing was happening in front of the platform and the large retractable door. Tom asked the security man to speed up the digital recording a little and suddenly they saw a truck parked there.

"Can you rewind that a bit?" Tom asked.

The picture restarted from the moment the truck pulled in front of the loading dock.

"That's the same truck that's out there now," Stockton observed.

Tom nodded and kept staring at the monitor. The driver's side door opened and a man came out wearing jeans and a black sweatshirt. On the back they could all clearly read DECO DECORATOR.

"I don't think that's Schroller," Stockton said right away.

They couldn't see the man's face until he walked around the front of the truck toward the passenger door. Still, it didn't look like Schroller and seeing the black hair and mustache didn't excite anyone in the room. The passenger door opened and when Isabelle stepped out, everyone yelled something.

"Yes! I was right! She's here!" Tom yelled. "Get the recording from inside."

The security manager was already bringing that up and matched the time stamp with the previous recording. Although he still did not recognize Schroller, Tom clearly saw Isabelle being pushed into the area with a gun to her back.

"Did he have an accomplice?" he asked Stockton.

"Not that I know," he said, shaking his head. "We only saw him."

On screen, Schroller suddenly grabbed a blanket and turned. He was staring straight at the camera and the security manager stopped the picture and enlarged it.

"Shit, it's Schroller. He's wearing a wig and a mustache. Damn, I've got to tell Marco at Sotheby's."

Tom called Marco while the manager continued playing the tape and then everything went dark.

"He covered up the camera," Frank said.

Tom was waiting for Marco to pick up when finally he heard a voice.

"O'Grady, is that you?" Tom asked.

"Yes, Marco's been shot. Nothing too serious I hope, but we're taking care of him. Schroller's shot him."

"I was just calling to tell you that he's disguised with a black . . ."

"We know," O'Grady said. "That's how he was able to get in."

"Did you get him?"

"Not yet, but we're closing in on him. Any lead on Isabelle?"

"Still looking, but we know she's here somewhere. We just watched a surveillance video. I'll call you later," Tom said ending the call, looking at everyone in the room.

"All right, the shooting has started at Sotheby's. Schroller got in. Let's hurry back to the loading dock," Tom said, feeling confident they'd find Isabelle.

When they got to the large loading dock area, Tom and the security guard started to move stacks of folded boxes and huge rolls of bubble wrapping. The cops and Stockton were doing the same at another wall.

"There's got to be a hiding place in here somewhere," Tom said.

Stockton had walked to the back wall next to the office and noticed that the floor was cleaner next to a double-wide stack of blankets. The stack reached almost to the ceiling and only by ladder would anyone have been able to stack them so neatly.

"Tom, take a look at this," he said.

Tom ran over. He knew right away that one stack had been moved on top of the other two. There had to be something hiding behind these, he thought.

"That's it!" Tom yelled, "Pull them down."

With blankets flying and unfolding as they were being pulled down from the two stacks, Tom noticed the top of a door jamb.

"There's a room behind these blankets, hurry," he yelled, as everyone was pulling more blankets down until they had uncovered the whole door. Tom pulled and pushed on the door handle, but it didn't budge. Frank moved Tom aside.

"Step back a second," he said.

He slammed the bottom of his boot on the handle from an angle and with such force, that it snapped off and the door opened slightly.

Tom rushed in and on a closed toilet seat he saw a wide eyed Isabelle. Her wrists were tied behind her back, and her ankles and legs were taped to the toilet bowl. Tom saw the tape on her mouth and he didn't hesitate. He yanked it off as fast as he could.

"Isabelle!" he yelled.

"Tom," she cried out with tears in her eyes.

While everyone stepped back a little, Tom hugged Isabelle and briefly kissed her on the mouth.

"Let's get you out of here," he said, trying to rip the duct tape away. Joanne was cutting the tape from around Isabelle's ankles. The cop gave her some support as she walked out into the loading dock area. Seeing Dr. Stockton, knowing that he was free too, Isabelle started crying.

"Shh. You're safe now," Tom said, holding her gently, remembering that he needed to be careful with her arm.

He took her left hand and turned it palm up. On the upper arm he saw the marks.

"Does it hurt?"

"Like hell. But don't worry. Did he get the painting?"

"No. I had Marco take the painting to Sotheby's. Schroller's already there and there's a shooting battle going on right now.

"No way! Damn, Tom, what time is it? The auction must have started."

"Don't worry about that auction."

"Why shouldn't I worry about it, aren't you?"

"I'll explain later, let's go to Sotheby's. They probably have him by now."

CHAPTER 39

Friday Afternoon—3:15 PM

M ARCO SAT ON the floor, waiting for the medic team to come and take care of the detective and himself. The detective was lying in an office and a policeman was pressing below the collarbone to stop the bleeding. He had coughed up a bit of blood and O'Grady worried that the man's lung had been hit. Having to chase after Schroller with the other cops, O'Grady had left as soon as he knew his colleague was alive and would probably make it.

Marco stared at the hole in his pants and the huge stain of blood below it. He had made himself a tourniquet to stop the bleeding and it seemed to be working, though his leg was hurting badly. Sitting in the hallway, he was listening to the bidding going on in the background. He could barely make out the amounts, but he was sure that at one point he had heard something like ten million. If they could hold off Schroller and find Isabelle, Tom would be a happy fellow, Marco thought. He was moving himself to a better position when suddenly Schroller appeared at the end of the hallway again. This time Schroller wasn't looking sideways as he intended to go into another room. Marco didn't hesitate and had just enough time to get off a shot. He couldn't tell whether he had hit him or not. All he heard was the closing of a door.

Schroller had to change direction, and had to go back to the ground floor before heading up again. Two of his access points to the room were very much guarded and he was on the way to a third. Someone had hit him in the shoulder, because there was blood on his fingertips when he felt where it hurt. He was sure it was only a surface wound and not something that would get in the way of him achieving his final quest.

He found another stairwell to the second floor and moved toward the sound of the bidding. It was quiet from time to time, but he was sure he had heard at least twelve million from the auction room.

He walked from one office to an adjacent one and looked through a window in the door into a hallway. This time the cops guarding a door had their backs to him. They were tempting targets, but did not want to alert others. He quietly stepped out of the office and moved on. It was quiet except for the bidding. Schroller couldn't believe this. These rich people were so full of themselves that all they were focused on was getting that painting. Not even the shooting fazed them. He shook his head and moved across the hallway to another room. He knew that this one gave him access to a client room where buyers were ushered in after a sale. The client room was the third access point to the auction room. He'd put an end to this ridiculous auction in a hurry, he thought.

He looked around and didn't see anyone. Just as he entered the empty office, he heard a door open. O'Grady had caught up with him.

CHAPTER 40

Friday Afternoon—3:20 PM

TOM, ISABELLE AND Stockton arrived at Sotheby's and Tom parked behind an ambulance. He ran up to one of the medics and asked if he could take a look at Isabelle's arm.

"I've got to take care of shooting victims inside, sorry," the man replied.

"Just please take a look at it, and tell us what she needs to do." Tom said.

The man turned to Isabelle who had her arm stretched toward him and the two marks were clearly visible. The centers were mostly white with black and brown specs in them. Around the wounds, a light red halo was clearly visible.

"Third degree burns, a few days old," the man said. "We'll take care of you after we're done here, or wait for another team to arrive."

"Thanks," Isabelle said.

"Stay here in the lobby. I'm going up to the auction room," Tom said.

"Do you think they have him by now? There are still a lot of police cars outside."

"I'm sure they do," Tom said, starting to move toward the doors off the lobby.

"I'm coming with you," Isabelle said.

Tom held the door open for the medic and Isabelle while Stockton went to the elevator.

"You guys go on," he said. "I'm going to the 9th floor. Dr. Amado is probably there with the curators."

"Good," Tom said. "Let's meet in the lobby in about a half hour."

In the waiting room Tom looked through the kitchen area connected to the room and then suddenly saw Marco sitting on the floor. Tom ran to him ahead of the medic.

"Marco, what happened?"

"The bastard shot me in the leg. I'm going to be okay though. Just a flesh wound," Marco said calmly and then turned to the medic while pointing to a room across the hallway. "You need to go to the detective in that room over there first. I'm sure he's worse off."

Tom stepped aside and Isabelle bent over and hugged Marco.

"Wow, it's good to see you," Marco said. "Now the only thing we have to deal with is Schroller. He's shooting up the place."

"You mean they haven't arrested him yet?" Tom asked surprised.

"I'm sure they're closing in on him, but nothing has come over the radio yet. O'Grady and several cops are chasing him."

"Are they closing in on him near the auction room?" Tom asked.

"As far as I know. By the way, even through all this, that auction is still going on. Your fortune is growing every minute," Marco said.

"I'm not worried about the auction," Tom said, picking up Marco's gun.

"Hey, leave that here. You've done well so far. Now stay away from Schroller! They'll get him any minute."

Tom tucked the gun in his belt anyway, knowing that Marco couldn't stop him.

"Don't worry. I just need to see Jonathan Metzer," Tom lied.

"Who's that?"

"He's the director."

"There was a guy in a suit who joined O'Grady when he went on without me."

"Let's go," Tom said and ran off, taking Isabelle's hand.

"Stay out of the way!" Marco yelled, but Tom and Isabelle had already turned the corner, heading for Metzer's office.

"Why do you want to go see him?" Isabelle asked Tom as they ran toward a set of offices.

"I'll explain it when we see him," Tom said. "What's the fastest way to his office?"

"Follow me, there's a shortcut through another office on the second floor," Isabelle said, and she lead him to the stairway.

On the second floor, Isabelle and Tom ran into the office of one of Metzer's assistants. There wasn't anybody in the office or in the adjoining office. They were right next to the client room now and they could hear the bidding loud and clear.

"Let's go to the auction room," Tom insisted, but Isabelle sensed danger.

"That's where Schroller's about to get to if they haven't caught him. He's probably waiting for the right moment to get the painting. Listen, the bidding has gone to twenty million."

"Fine, but we need to find Jonathan," Tom said as he moved into another office. He suddenly stopped as he saw a secretary hiding under her desk.

"What the . . . ," Tom started saying, as the secretary shook her head and motioned to the opened door.

Isabelle had her back to the adjacent office. Tom was too late to warn her. He had seen real fear on the secretary's face and he was sure she was telling him that there was someone else in that room. Tom tried to warn Isabelle by crying out her name, but it was too late. Schroller jumped from behind the door and grabbed Isabelle. Immediately he held the machine gun to her head.

"How did you get here, bitch?" he asked, stepping into the room. Tom stood still as if frozen to the ground.

"You!" Schroller said. "You never learn, do you?"

"Let her go," Tom said. "The place is full of cops. There's no way you can get out. You can forget that painting now."

"Tommy boy, go get that painting now or I'll blow her head off. You've got a half a minute."

"There's an auction going on. I can't just walk in there and take it away."

"Twenty million dollars for a lousy painting?" Schroller asked, commenting on the voice coming from the auction room. "Your thirty seconds have started already!"

Tom decided not to go through the double door of the client room, but chose the hallway. He was glad he did because he ran into a cop, followed by O'Grady and Metzer.

"Tom, what the hell?" O'Grady asked, totally surprised to see Tom.

"He's got Isabelle again. I've got to get the painting."

"We knew he was in there. Damn, another hostage situation. I don't know how you do it, Tom!"

"Hey, I've got no time to argue, he's given me thirty seconds."

"I'll get the painting," Metzer said, leaving right away.

"He's not leaving here alive," O'Grady said. "Where is the bastard?"

Tom motioned them to follow him. In the office, Schroller had not moved. His finger was on the trigger and he warned them right away.

"This time I'm going to get that Rembrandt."

"Okay, but don't do anything stupid," O'Grady said, raising his hands a little. "Someone went to get the painting."

"You've got ten seconds or I'll blow her head off," Schroller snapped.

At that moment, Metzer walked in with the packaged painting and pushed it along the desk toward Schroller. From the other side of the room, the bidding now had gone to twenty five million.

"What the hell are they bidding on in there?" he asked.

"Just another painting," Jonathan blurted out.

"Great, let's go see. I may get a nice bonus after all," Schroller said and pushed the barrel of the gun deeper into Isabelle's cheek.

"You," he ordered her, "Pick up the painting."

Once Isabelle had the painting, Schroller pulled her back, keeping the gun firmly in place. Slowly, he eased toward the client room where he had direct access to the auction room. Tom took a step forward, but O'Grady spread out his arms, holding everyone back. Schroller continued moving toward the client room and was quickly out of sight. O'Grady grabbed his phone and pushed a few buttons. Behind him, Tom pulled Jonathan's jacket sleeve, almost dragging him into the hallway.

"Show me the closest entrance to the room," Tom demanded.

"Come with me," Jonathan whispered to Tom.

Before O'Grady saw them, Tom and Jonathan were running as fast as they could to a small door.

"This is the access door we use to bring in the items to be auctioned," Jonathan said, still whispering. "I'll get O'Grady and the detective, wait here."

Jonathan ran back, but Tom entered the room quietly. The bidding noise was loud and he heard twenty seven million. Tom ran as fast as he could to the double door he expected Schroller and Isabelle to come through from the client room. As he got to the door, Schroller had just kicked it open behind him, still facing into the client room in case anyone might come after him. One more swift kick and the double door swung open. Tom hid behind one of the opened doors. Schroller was holding Isabelle, the gun firmly pressed against her temple now. He backed up slowly into the auction room. Just before he turned, Tom took Marco's gun out of his belt, and leveled it high, stepping from behind the door. Although he was shaking a little, he was determined to shoot Schroller straight in the head.

The bid suddenly went to thirty million and Schroller apparently couldn't believe it. Curious, he turned around, taking the gun away from Isabelle's head. The next moment, he was totally amazed. His jaw dropped as he faced an empty room except for a pair of loudspeakers announcing the bids.

It all happened within a few seconds, but it was plenty of time for Tom to take advantage of the surprise. He stepped right behind Schroller, never wavering, the gun firmly in his hands. He jabbed the gun barrel in the back of Schroller's head. During his step forward, he had nudged Isabelle to the side. He yelled at Schroller.

"Drop the gun! Now! This is the end of the road, you son of a bitch."

Schroller lowered the gun a little and started to turn around.

"You'll never shoot! You can't beat me," he teased Tom.

Just before he raised the gun again, O'Grady and the detective burst through the same small door Tom had come through. With their guns drawn, they rushed to Schroller and in seconds they were in front of him. Seeing no way out, he dropped the machine gun.

"Raise your hands," Tom ordered Schroller.

There was smile on Tom's face. The gun was no longer steady in his hand.

O'Grady grabbed Schroller's arms and put them behind his back. The detective handcuffed him immediately. Tom lowered the gun as Isabelle threw herself into his arms. Tom hugged her tightly.

After Schroller was led away, Jonathan turned off the tape recorder that was still running.

"I think we were at the end of that tape. We didn't record anything more," he laughed. "Timing is everything in our business."

Tom and Isabelle smiled. Heading for the main door, Marco came limping in with the help of a cop.

"I can't believe it worked. You stopped him!" Marco exclaimed.

"Yes, he did," Isabelle answered, putting her arm around Tom.

"You know, it should have been me," Marco said. "I was supposed to help you with this menace. I'm the cop."

"Ex-cop," Tom laughed. "Anyway, it worked because I had your gun. Here, it's all yours, I never fired it."

Marco took the gun and put it in his belt.

"What happened to the auction? Everyone clear the room in a hurry?"

"Yeah, what was going on here?" Isabelle chimed in.

"There never was an auction," Tom explained. "A few days ago I made a deal with the Metropolitan that I would loan the painting to them for a good sum of money each year. We just kept the plan for the auction alive, in case we needed to lure Schroller here if all else failed. Of course, he was supposed to be arrested outside before he came in, but he fooled a few people."

Tom threw a quick look at O'Grady.

"By doing all that you put Isabelle at risk," O'Grady said.

"If he was going to kill her, he would have done so earlier. I think that whoever hired him told him to use as much pressure as possible without killing anyone."

"You might be right," O'Grady said. "But I've got one detective seriously wounded. He better make it."

"Let's hope so," Isabelle said.

Downstairs in the conference room, Isabelle's arm was being bandaged up when Dr. Amado walked in. After checking that Isabelle was fine, he turned to Tom with an outstretched hand.

"Mr. Arden, thanks. You saved a great painting."

"Glad to do it, sir. I can still stop by in the morning and settle things right?

"Stop worrying about money young man. All is taken care of," he said and slapped Tom shoulder.

Tom walked over to Marco who was lying on a stretcher, ready to be taken to an ambulance.

"Thanks, man. Sorry you took a bullet for it. I hope you can make it next week."

"What's going on next week?"

"I'm throwing a party for all my clients. Time to settle up," Tom said as they walked alongside the gurney. Marco nodded and looked up at Tom.

"Good decision. It's about time!"

Isabelle put her arm around Tom's waist.

"Yes, Tom. It's so good to be free again. Thanks for your quick thinking," she said kissing him on the cheek.

"You can thank me later," Tom smiled, squeezing her closer to him.

"There's one thing though, when you slowed the drop down, Schroller was really pissed and look what he did," she said lifting up her arm. "There never was a choice between me and the painting right?"

"Of course not, but I admit, I did have a hard time giving up that painting, but when it was worthless it was really easy."

"Only then?" she asked, poked him in the side and smiled. "Glad you timed it right."

As Marco was put in the ambulance, he took Tom's arm and brought him closer so Tom had to bend down.

"You've done well in the end. Your dad would have been proud of you," he said as Isabelle also got into the ambulance.

"All right, let's get you two to the hospital for some proper care," Tom said, gently stomping his fist on Marco's shoulder.

"Hey, take it easy," Marco said. "You're dealing with an old man here."

Tom choked a little and looked Marco in the eyes.

"I know. You're the old man I missed in my life."

Düsseldorf, Germany

THE QUIET OF the old neighborhood in Unterrath was shattered by dozens of police cars with sirens blaring. A woman walking her small dog on the sidewalk covered her ears. As each car pulled up near the front of a gated mansion, the noise died down and was replaced by the slamming of car doors. And as suddenly as the noise had interrupted the peaceful area, the quiet returned. The woman stood still and stared as several policemen opened the black iron gate and ran to the front door.

A lieutenant with the police rang the doorbell and took an envelope out of his pocket. After a few moments, the door slowly opened half way. A gray haired man leaned into the opening.

"*Guten Tag. Womit kann ich Ihnen dienen?*" he asked calmly.

The lieutenant slapped the envelope in the palm of his left hand.

"I have a search warrant here. Are you the owner?"

"No, I'm the butler. Wait here, I'll call him," the man said and closed the door.

One of the policemen raised his eyebrows.

"Is he coming back?"

"Of course, we just wait," the lieutenant said and smiled.

A few moments later a man came to the door and like the previous man, opened it half way.

"Are you Drexler?" the lieutenant asked.

"Yes, I am," Drexler said. "I've got nothing to do with the police. Perhaps it's my son you need."

"No, you'll do fine," the lieutenant said.

At the same time, a policeman pushed the door open further and several entered the house, pushing Drexler to the side.

"What is the meaning of this?" he asked.

"We have a search warrant. We believe you have stolen property on these premises."

"I protest. We're upstanding citizens. Everything we have is ours!" Drexler protested.

"Here is the document, signed by the judge and according to the *Strafprozeßordnung*," the lieutenant said, handing the envelope to Drexler. He motioned for more policemen to enter the house.

"Search every room, every cabinet and look for hidden places, understood?" he asked the men. Most of them didn't bother answering but went into the house with gusto. It wasn't every day they got to see how the rich lived.

Every room downstairs and the basement were searched in minute detail. After each room was completed, one member of the team would report back to the lieutenant. After two hours, nothing had been found downstairs and Drexler demanded again that they leave.

Moving the whole operation upstairs, a team came upon the large parlor that served as a study room. They felt, pulled and pushed wood panels and every metal fixtures. One of the policemen was about to ask for a floor plan of the house because he thought something was odd about the layout. Suddenly, as he was pushing an ornate box on a shelf, part of a wall gave way and became the doorway into a great room. Inside he turned on a switch. The room had very low lighting. The reason became immediately clear as he looked around the room at the walls. The lieutenant had joined him in the room and looked on in amazement.

There were so many paintings that all the walls were covered from top to bottom.

"This is what we were looking for," he said. "There must be over a hundred."

He took his flashlight for a closer inspection of the masterpieces before him. He read the signatures on the paintings and labels on the frames. He moved his light slowly from one painting to the next, stopping at each one briefly. Every time he stopped he read the name of each artist aloud, Memling, Durer, Van Eyck, van Gogh, Monet, Rubens, Rembrandt . . .